Humphrey Joseph Desmond

**Outlooks and Insights**

In behalf of larger and more hopeful views of life

Humphrey Joseph Desmond

**Outlooks and Insights**
*In behalf of larger and more hopeful views of life*

ISBN/EAN: 9783337250317

Printed in Europe, USA, Canada, Australia, Japan

Cover: Foto ©Andreas Hilbeck / pixelio.de

More available books at **www.hansebooks.com**

# Outlooks

## and Insights.

In Behalf of Larger and More
Hopeful Views of Life.

By Humphrey J. Desmond.

*"Care not, while we hear*
*A  trumpet  in  the  distance pealing news*
*Of  better, and  Hope, a poising eagle, burns*
*Above the unrisen morrow."*
—TENNYSON.

———

NEW YORK    CHICAGO
D. H. McBRIDE & CO., PUBLISHERS,
1899.

# CONTENTS.

PAGE.

ABOVE THE SORDID—   -   -   -   -   7

Ossification.  -   -   -   -   -   -   7
Side Lines.   -   -   -   -   -   8
What a Monk Wrote.  -   -   -   -   8
Keep Sweet.  -   -   -   -   -   -   9
An Un-austere Saint.  -   -   -   10
A Happy Disposition.  -   -   -   12
Seeing Life.  -   -   -   -   13

AS A MAN LIVES—   -   -   -   -   16

The Ruling Passion.  -   -   -   16
Small Vices.  -   -   -   -   -   17
Even Worldlings See It.  -   -   -   18
Sane Insanities.  -   -   -   -   18
The Anti-Social Feeling.  -   -   20
Turning Points.  -   -   -   -   21

THE PHILOSOPHY OF MODERATION—  -   24

The Flying Years.  -   -   -   -   24
Would We Live Our Lives Over Again?  -   26
Something Must be Missed.  -   -   27
A False Aim.  -   -   -   -   28
The Measure of Success.  -   -   -   30

SPIRITUAL FORCE—   -   -   -   -   33

The Will To Do.  -   -   -   -   33
Be Just and Fear Not.  -   -   -   34
The Kernel of Progress.  -   -   -   37

COURAGE OF CONVICTION—  -   -   -   40

In the Living Present.  -   -   -   40
Right, Rather than Popularity.  -   41
"Respectable" Opinions.  -   -   -   42
Avant Couriers.  -   -   -   -   44
The Brave Man Chooses.  -   -   -   46

# CONTENTS.

|  | PAGE. |
|---|---|
| Now is the Appointed Time— | 48 |
| Get Into Action. | 48 |
| To-morrow and To-morrow and To-morrow. | 49 |
| Action is Power. | 50 |
| The Society of the Energetic— | 52 |
| Daring to Do. | 52 |
| The Discipline of Mind. | 53 |
| Prescience. | 54 |
| The Opportune Moment. | 56 |
| Suaviter in Modo— | 60 |
| Serenity. | 60 |
| Morbid Periods. | 62 |
| The Impolicy of Quarrels. | 63 |
| The Art of Persuasion. | 65 |
| The Point of View— | 67 |
| The Poet's Eye. | 67 |
| The Habit of Satire. | 69 |
| Shapes of Vice. | 71 |
| Not All One Way. | 73 |
| The Wisdom of Our Elders. | 74 |
| Perspectives— | 76 |
| Narrow-Guage Statesmen. | 76 |
| Radicalism. | 78 |
| Time for the Puritan. | 79 |
| A Lesson in Public Spirit. | 81 |
| "Only a Sentiment." | 83 |
| Attitudes— | 86 |
| Power in Repose. | 86 |
| One's Own Individuality. | 87 |
| Signs of Character. | 88 |
| Recurrences— | 92 |
| New Causes. | 92 |
| "Paramount Rights." | 95 |
| Lost Arts. | 97 |
| Reverence. | 99 |

4

# CONTENTS.

PAGE.

THE KNOWLEDGE OF EVIL— -   •    •    101

    A Question of Innocence.   •    •    101
    An Apostolic Caution.   •    •    •  102
    Degenerate Tendencies.   •    •    103
    The Black Art.   •    •    •    105

ENLARGING VISTAS—   •    •    •    108

    The Unfinished Bible.   •    •    108
    Hush! Hush!   •    •    •    109
    In God's Time.   •    •    111
    "Think Ye?"   •    •    112
    Theological Insularity.   •    •    114
    Ideas in the Pulpit.   •    •    116
    Repairs on the Church.   •    •    118

THE GOSPEL FOR THE POOR—   •    •    121

    Moral Sanitation.   •    •    121
    The Poor We Have Always With Us.   •    123
    A Civilization of Water.   •    •    125
    After Dinner Charity.   •    •    126
    Mediæval Charity.   •    •    128
    Education in Giving.   •    •    130
    Brains and Heart.   •    •    132

AMERICANISM—   •    •    •    134

    What is Americanism?   •    •    134
    A Matter of Environment.   •    •    137
    Beyond Their Station.   •    •    139
    Rise in the World.   •    •    143

THE PEOPLE KING—   •    •    147

    Ordinary People.   •    •    147
    A Lesson in Ethics.   •    •    149
    Level Up.   •    •    •    151

THE HARD FACTS—   •    •    155

    A Balance of Power.   •    •    155
    The Boycott Family.   •    •    157
    Cannot Use the Church.   •    •    159

# Outlooks and Insights.

## ABOVE THE SORDID.

Ossification. WHEN we grow old the veins and arteries harden. The muscles grow stiff. The lungs and the heart are clogged with limy deposits. If some means could be discovered to rid the body of waste material, or some diet followed which would throw less work upon the excretory organs, most of us might reach the century mark.

But we also ossify in our minds and in our souls. While there are experiences in life which chasten and purify —and sorrow which does not crush, is one of these—there are routines in life, ways of living and sordid aims which destroy every God-given sympathy, rob the mind of all its generous impulses, cramp the soul and drive all poetry and beauty out of life. What does the social or political or pecuniary success, which leaves us thus ossified in brain and soul, amount to? To be hard of heart,

7

calculating of mind and iron-willed, is simply a condition of moral death.

Side Lines. MRS. BROWNING in one of her poems says:

"Let us be content in work,
    To do the thing we can and not presume
    To fret because 'tis little."

There is, however, a chance for every one, no matter what may be the ordinary duties of life, to develop little interests aside from avocations by which one's living is earned. In his Wilhelm Meister, Goethe says: "One ought every day, at least, to hear a little song, read a good poem, see a fine picture, and, if it were possible, speak a few reasonable words." Some people are so happily constituted that they are able to go out of their way to do an act of kindness every day.

What a Monk Wrote. A MONK wrote these lines away back in the "dark ages," when, it is alleged, that monks did nothing but segregate:

"Count that day lost
    Whose low descending sun
    Views from your hand
    No worthy action done."

What St. Bernard wrote, old John Brown, of Ossowatomie, taught to his

children, and Wendell Phillips copied
in a thousand autograph albums.

The sentiment is good, wholesome
and instructive. Each day has its
duties, be they little or great. That
which we esteem the least may turn
out to be the most important. Sometimes a single word comes up to St.
Bernard's idea of a worthy action.
Sometimes it is a chance lift volun-
teered to one in difficulty. Sometimes
it is a good resolution. Sometimes it
is a temptation resisted. The field is
broad and open to all. Everybody may
write the monk's lines in his memoran-
dum book.

Keep
Sweet. OUR Christianity ought to enable us
to come up after the struggles and disappointments and crosses of each day,
sweet tempered and smiling. It makes
a great difference with our career and
it makes a great difference with our
character.

The "slings and arrows of outrageous
fortune" glance off the smooth sur-
faced temper of him who preserves his
digestion and his merriment and his
courtesy even when matters seem to go

adversely and difficulties are impending.

Earnestness is good and gravity is good, but not at the expense of Christian kindness. And Christian kindness should exist not as an act of penance, but as the spontaneous expression of a healthy character. The poet cries

"Give me the man who sings at his work."

And give us the Christian associates who, after their work is done, are neither dull nor irritable nor indolent, but who have a wish for the bright things of life (while there is faith in them) and an irradiating vital good temper.

The will to cultivate such a temper is gradually served by the habit until it becomes second nature; so that a happy disposition—upon which so much of the enjoyment of life depends—is quite as much a matter of acquisition as a gift of nature.

An Un-Austere Saint. "HE was gay, genial and irresistibly winning." Words spoken of St. Philip Neri, who walked the streets of Rome some three hundred years ago.

Sad people went out of their way to meet him, for the sight of his face made them happy. It is said that after his death, depressed people went to his room to have their hearts raised. His presence was sunshine. His very look calmed troubled souls. His words inspired confidence. His step was the signal of good cheer.

All this is quite credible. It should seem plausible to us in these days when there is belief in personal magnetism. Have we not all observed in a less degree the influence, either for gladness or depression, of certain individualities?

What a power for good a man gifted as was St. Phillip Neri might be. How much better employed is this happy endowment when it is devoted to the welfare of one's fellow Christians rather than to winning office or trade. St. Phillip Neri was eighty years of age when he died, and at his death and all through his life we may believe that he gained more satisfaction in using his great gifts in diffusing happiness, than if he had ruled the Papal court or sat as a prince among Venetian merchants.

A Happy
Disposition. LIFE in its totality is both sad and glad. But it is gladder and brighter with those who determine to make it so. A happy disposition is worth half one's fortune in life. Things do seem to come out right in the end for those who look away from the gloom, keep up their courage and trust to the good time coming and the kind Providence that watches over all.

If we study the processes of the mind, we begin to be more and more persuaded that nothing in life is irremediable or irretrievable. Time seems to cure the deepest afflictions. The worries of yesterday are trifles to the memory of to-morrow. A merciful Creator has so constituted us that we rise from the profoundest grief to bear with fortitude the saddest bereavements. A lost love finds balm in the treasure house of the future. What seems the awful decree of Fate, which rives hearts and makes the years to come seem black and bleak and cold and desolate, is less awful and less tragic as the months roll on. Men smile again, though their fortunes are broken, though poverty succeeds affluence, and though obscurity follows power. Every cloud has a silver lining. The darkest hour is the hour before the dawn.

These considerations and this knowledge of the recuperative power of the mind, advise us of the good sense of looking on the bright side. Let us raise our hearts. We may be happy yet. The sun is still shining, if we but get in the sunlight. Returning seasons still new flowers bring. After all, 'tis a good old world to live in. And our faith is that we were created to be happy, and not to be miserable in it.

So much of the unhappiness of life comes from being morbid over afflictions and crosses. It is the mistake of looking on the gloomy side only. The evil of the bereavement and the sadness, are deepened by brooding, and the sorrow sometimes leads to catastrophe and tragedy. What is needed are physicians of the mind to prescribe diversion, hard work, new interests, and more sunlight.

Seeing Life. A FAMOUS German writer has aptly said, "You must treat a work of art like a great man. Stand before it, and wait patiently till it deigns to speak."

In the art galleries people stand for a long time before some famous painting. New beauties and finer lines are constantly revealed to them. It has taken the artist a long time to execute his great work. He has put his heart and soul into the creation, and we cannot expect to appreciate or understand it if we simply give it a passing glance.

If there are hidden meanings in life we do not see them by haste in any manner—whether in hurried travel or in eager pursuit of wealth. There are more beauties—there is more "soul"— in the relations cultivated by a good Christian life and in the duties it involves than can be revealed in the greatest work of art. The painter, after some years of labor, exhibits his masterpiece on canvas. But the active and useful life of twenty or forty years has its masterpiece in the character formed and developed; and one may see in its acts and its thoughts, its self-denials and its heroism, something more admirable than any art gallery possesses.

Let us not hurry through the corridors of time without appreciating what is good and true and beautiful in character, and let us develop those human sympathies and that Christian faith that give life its nobility.

THE blacksmith's arm is developed to a fine proportion because he uses it; the dancer's leg or the cycler's calf comes to be, what it is, by use. The blood flows where it is called. As with the muscles, so with the brain.

If the brain is used to write poetry, the brain development is poetic; if to plan benevolence, it takes on the benevolent aspect, even to the face. If we think good thoughts we show them in our faces; if evil thoughts, depravity looks out of our eyes—and with the strength of these parts, grows the disposition as well as the facility.

Gamblers so attune their nervous systems that they cannot be comfortable unless they are playing at some game of chance for some stake. The lecher is sent along by his insane wit to the excitements and incitements of libertinism. This is what is meant by the expression, "possessed by one's sin," "the ruling passion strong in death." It is a fearful fact, not fully realized until men are in the maelstrom of their own evil natures. A man thus builds up the tendency of his own life by the way he lives it. And as he lives, so is he apt to die.

**Small Vices.** THE average man is not a bad fellow. His vices are usually the small vices. He does not see them himself in their pettiness. Few men act on the philosopher's *summa* of human wisdom: "know thyself." They can't perceive their weak vanity, their sneaking lust or their mean avarice; simply because the outcroppings are in small and not in gross vices.

Society is sometimes shocked by the fall of men currently held in high esteem. It is wondered how one of such heretofore irreproachable life could thus sin. But the answer is found in the existence of small vices. They who pinched the poor of their dues were already far advanced in dishonesty, and they who went voyaging out upon the sea of a guilty imagination were already whited sepulchres of corruption.

**Even Worldlings See It.** MEN of evil lives are not wise to plan or shrewd in action. "A heart to resolve, a head to contrive and a hand to execute" co-exist only in those who live in accordance with right mental, moral and physical laws.

The old saying, "Whom the gods destroy they first drive mad," means that those who encounter wreck and ruin are chiefly responsible for it themselves. Their evil temper, their reckless actions and their foolish vagaries constitute their madness.

A sensualist is never a good business man. A drunkard is a poor politician. A libertine is always a social failure. Any moral weakness corrupts the whole mental and physical system.

> "Errors in morals breed errors in the brain,
> And these, reciprocally, these again."

In the great affairs of life all wise decision and prudent action should ·be based on right living. The mental and moral vision should be normal. Nerves should be natural and the environment wholesome. Otherwise we labor under the stress of unwise circumstances.

**Sane Insanities.** SOME experts on the question of insanity hold that there are kinds of sanity more disagreeable, dangerous and anti-social than some of the insanities cooped up in asylums.

Where avarice and miserliness run in a family, resulting in sordid lives, rack-renting landlords and bitter family feuds over property, it is a question whether this is not a curse both to the family and to the community infested by such a family, far worse than mental imbecility or the tendency to senile dementia.

There are some families which spawn their progeny upon society with the inevitable consequence that the sons must "sow their wild oats" before they settle down to decent living. In the process, there are saddened homes, broken hearts and ruined lives. This species of heredity moral unsoundness is a worse infliction on society, and perhaps a worse heritage to the individuals concerned, than actual mental instability.

What of the cranks, the hopelessly impracticables, the fanatics, the bigots, and *id genus omne?* They are all inflictions upon society and all measurably victims of a deformed mental or moral constitution—although their deformity is not actual insanity.

Christianity, in the mild, even tempered and kind spirit of its Great Founder, is the true sanitary force tending to dissolve the mental and moral deformities that afflict society and to make us all gentlemen and gentlewomen in the true sense—considerate, kind, upright, with our angles rounded off and our idiosyncrasies smoothed away.

The "Anti-Social Feeling." INSANITY in its final analysis is an anti-social feeling—war against the saner usages and desires of the community.

Want of social sympathy is a mild form of insanity. The eccentric who growls at the approach of his fellow-man: the unneighborly who takes pleasure in being disagreeable: the socially isolated who repels rather than attracts communication, are of this class.

Easy associations with one's neighbors, affability of expression and smoothness of manner denote sanity. Pleasant greetings, the taking of a per-

sonal interest in others, congeniality
of companionships, politeness, defer-
ence and courtesy are qualities which fit
people rightfully in the social sphere.
Society gives such people strength, and
they in turn strengthen society.

Turning
Points.
WE all reach turning points in life—
times when events and reasons concur
in urging a change of course—possibly
a complete reversal of our previous
direction, possibly a turning off from
former aims to newer ends which seem
to us wiser and better.

Under the influence of certain
motives a man has concluded that his
happiness lies in attaining special conditions — such as a fair degree of
wealth, or eminence in a profession, or
the applause of his village as an orator,
or a pleasant home life, or a political
position. But along in the toil of
attainment a higher wisdom than that
of his youth comes to him, and what
was gilded seems now paltry, and what
he thought of with a zest now seems a
barren ideality.

These turning points come too, in
conviction, and habits and ways of

living. Not merely does the liberal become the conservative; but the partisanships of earlier years mellow into the charitable, considerate and judicial opinions of middle life. The most positive men are continually learning something new, veering ever so slightly in their views, tiring even of their own iterations.

Rays of light coming through change of environment, through the lessons of sorrow, or through a variety of other inspiring causes lead men to give up the pursuit of false gods and turn toward purer purposes. In this process, the turn in life may be of a more or less drastic character. In the story of the saints we read of men giving their wealth to the poor and forsaking the world, as a means of divesting themselves of the clogs which held them to a state of life from which they craved freedom. They burned the ships of their old world behind them, so to speak—there could be no turning back. To regain bodily health men have given up business and broken up their homes; why not similar sacrifices, to regain moral health, although, perhaps the reward is greater to win the battle on the ground, without retreat. To entrench against impending failure in business, men háve braved the loss of social prestige and denied themselves accustomed luxuries; why not like mortification to protect and safeguard character, honor and virtue? When it is thus reasoned we come to the "turning point"—implying the yielding up of what the heart has craved or what pleasant association has endeared or passion has coveted—these less worthy ends of existence, going by the board, to reach that greater success which a good life, with a clearer view, makes for.

# THE PHILOSOPHY OF MODERA-
# TION.

TWO score years or three score—the
difference is very slight in the eternity
of time—and the end is soon reached.
Up through the golden years of youth
there is anticipation; but the wealth
and success and position, for which men
labor, can be enjoyed but briefly. It
takes thirty or forty years of frugality
to acquire what is called "competence";
and competence can be possessed only
during the ten or twenty years when
most of us are on the down-grade of
life. We know all this, our attention
is frequently called to it; but yet there
is a zest in living. We find this a dear
old world—no other place like it—and
we are in no hurry to leave it. Even
old men racked with rheumatism,
bereft of teeth and with little in life to
anticipate and none of its illusions
remaining, are in no hurry to be
through with it. They see each new
summer sun rise and circle in its

meridian with an interest as grateful as that of their childhood.

That everything on earth is brief and transitory is no reason that life should be without enjoyment. That death is certain is no reason that we should stand always with the shadow of the tomb upon us.

Nature assuages the hardness of this fate by letting us forget it; and by prompting us to live on and hope on and enjoy each day as if life were to go on forever. If we take life in that way —and the mass of humanity in greater or less degree do so take it—we are taking it at its best.

But while we allow nature and a kind Providence to carry us along oblivious of doomsday, we shall also provide for our happiness by being wise enough to see that there is an end, and that violent passions and over-mastering ambitions are foolish, in view of the fewness of our years and the burden such travail puts upon us. In most instances that which embitters life, is disappointment resulting from placing two much stress upon the things of this world,—its wealth, its successes, or the pursuit of its pleasures. It might be well if those who have thought to find their heaven here, and are bitterly disappointed, could realize the heaven of the hereafter; but religion holds out little of such hope to the voluptuary, the miser and the worldling. Here in fact are the real life failures: they who for the prizes of this brief life let go the promises of eternity.

**Would we Live Our Lives Over Again?** SOMEBODY, writing in a current magazine, discusses the question: "Would we live our lives over again?"—just as they have been, of course. And the writer comes to the conclusion that, ask the question of the majority of Americans, and "they would answer 'I pass' even when holding a full hand."

Life and the new years coming to us seem pleasant because of the illusions, with which our imagination fills them. The sweetest pleasure, like the Hebrew verb, has no present tense. Unless we place our calculations within the limits of moderation and govern our desires by the higher motives of Christian philosophy, we are bound to be disappointed.

Observe the cases of Byron and Goethe—two men of genius and also votaries of pleasure. One would suppose that the former had a pleasant time of it here—"a short life and a merry one"; yet he would admit that he had only two days of genuine happiness out of it.

Goethe lived to die at eighty or more, and all he counted out of his years of breathing was eleven days of a good time.

"He who has supped at the table of kings
And yet starved in the sight of luxurious things;
Heard the music and yet missed the tune; who
    hath wasted
One part of life's grand possibilities—friend,
That man will bear with him, be sure, to the end,
A blighted experience, a rancor within.
You may call it a virtue—I call it a sin."

**Something Must Be Missed.** IT is all in the forecast, depending on whether you are the votary of pleasure and passion, as Owen Meredith shows himself in the above lines, or the ascetic and the wizard, as other men have been from choice,—following a philosophy expressly opposite.

Actual achievement in any worthy department of human exertion seems to enforce a measurable self-denial of

what are termed "the pleasures of life."
The earnest teacher, the zealous
preacher, the faithful jurist, the live
editor, the successful banker or mer-
chant, can not go and come to pleasant
climates with the flocking of the birds,
nor drink deep, nor turn night into day,
nor dance attendance on beauty, nor
shake care and responsibility.

Plain living is a condition for high
thinking. Devotion to one's specialty
is a necessity if any eminence is to be
gained in a life's work. Consecration
to the work of God in the experience of
the Catholic church requires the priest
to forego domestic ties. The illustrations are numerous. The poet and
the epicure may protest. The fact
remains.

A False
Aim. THERE is a familiar fable which
represents a knight in hot pursuit of a
receding phantom. Again and again
he stretches forth his arm to seize the
fleeting fraud. Again and again it
eludes him. So he spends fruitless
years and vain endeavors grasping at
expectation and realizing disappointment. The fable is varied, but the

moral remains the same, in the labor of Sispyhus, who rolls his great round stone up a moral incline only to see it roll down repeatedly when near the top; or in the hopeless task of "dropping buckets into empty wells and growing old in drawing nothing up."

What, with old Rome, was ease with dignity—*otium cum dignitate,* and what the modern Italians dream of as *dolce far niente,* a time of pleasant leisure, has been the aim in life of thousands of men. To get the means therefor, they have toiled all the day and troubled all the night; saying: "Some day wealth will buy this ease and comfort; some day a golden key will unlock the rare enjoyments of life." Carlyle says: 'Whoever has sixpence is sovereign over all men to the extent of that sixpence; commands cooks to feed him, philosophers to teach him, kings to mount guard over him—to the extent of that sixpence.' Let us, therefore, hoard up these very potent *genii* called sixpences. The more of them the better, and the further they will go and the more limitless will be their power.

So the man is transformed into the machine called Gathergold. Tennyson's hero in Locksley Hall utters a malediction upon this slavery of civilization when he curses the

"Social wants that sin against the strength of
    youth."

Too bad that the best time of life must be devoted to amassing merely that which will insure food and shelter to an old man. Youth is chained like Milton's Sampson,

"At the mill with slaves
Condemned to labor under Philistine yoke."

But the yoke is a voluntary one. The youth is like the knight in the fable. He has elected to pursue a fraudulent ideal in life. His tantalus leads him through all kinds of labor. When all is over he is too old to obtain the substantial worth of life.

**The Measure of Success.** WE are inclined to protest that money should not be the measure of success in life, yet all our modern biographers and all our modern novels, which are more or less expressive of the moral level of the time, are stamped with this notion of success. To say of a young man, "he is making a great deal of money,"-is a challenge for our respect and esteem. "He is growing rich," "his practice is worth thousands," "he is doing an immense business," "he has gotten hold of a gold mine," are translated to mean that he, whoever he may be, is getting the true value out of life.

When we come to think it over, we will reflect that all this money-gathering may co-exist with other conditions that do not promise happiness with wealth. One may make money and yet develop no character. Then the enjoyment of his wealth or the power that money confers belongs to somebody who takes or inherits from him. He may win wealth and lose health. He may pile up riches at the expense of his personal salvation, his truth, his honor. He may rise in the world, isolated from any genuine friendships or relationships.

Let it be granted that if a man makes much money and yet keeps his health, develops his character, retains his friends and saves his soul, he is truly successful. What proportion, think you, of those who amass wealth do this? Not one-tenth, we surmise. An Abbott Lawrence among Boston merchants is produced at the rate of two per generation. The effort to succeed notably and grandly, in other directions as well as in the money direction, break the man down if he tries it; but usually he does not try it, for his eagerness after money dwarfs his growth in character, deprives him of the privilege of friendship and endangers his soul.

# SPIRITUAL FORCE.

THE will to do the right as we see it is spiritual force; and spiritual energy is the best development of what is called "force of character." It is a thing of the mind, a matter of wishing and striving, strongly, deeply, continuously.

Passion is always playing across the purposes that our moral being puts forth. Men of good intention are thus veered from the straight course. "The spirit is willing but the flesh is weak" —which is the time-honored apology for want of spiritual force.

According to the old moralists the utterly reprobate are those who have not the will to turn from their besetting sins. They may, at times, repent, but are never sincerely resolved to give up their pleasures. The intellect of conscience remains, but its will is dead.

'That is the best blood which has the most iron in't
    To edge resolve with."

That is the true spiritual life which makes for the right with forceful determination. It is so earnest in its ends that it calls to its aid every assistance. Altogether, aside from any religious considerations, the influence of prayer, mortification and the avoidance of temptation must be recognized in the growth of spiritual force. From a purely psychological standpoint, fervent prayer is fervent wishing for the good resolved upon. It is an exercise and a formulation of spiritual force. The avoidance of temptation is the weakening of those passions which play across the moral purposes.

> "Refrain to-night.
> And that shall lend a kind of easiness
> To the next abstinence; the next more easy.
> For use almost can change the stamp of nature."

And mortification and self-denial still further strengthen the spiritual will. Thus, when the will to do right is strong, there is also clearer moral vision. Make-shifts, compromises, bribes of time and circumstance, are thrust aside and the man of spiritual force sees without hesitation that

> "If right be right, to follow right
> Were wisdom in the scorn of consequence."

**Be Just and Fear Not.** THERE is a strength about just conduct and the policy of justice itself that is commonly misprized. The judgment of many men is warped into believing that *finesse* is better than honesty, or that expedients and tricks are shrewder than straightforwardness.

If a victory is not predicated upon truth, it is barren, joyless and transitory. To take broad views is to look at matters as they transpire in the long run. In the long run the indirect, vacillating policy is rejected. In the long run the man of tricks and intrigues is well understood by his neighbors in the community, and his influence is discounted accordingly.

On the other hand—for an honest, consistent policy, presented openly and above board, there is generated a proper esteem. If it be sound and beneficial, it will eventually have its way. Similarly with the man of honest methods. His candor is respected; his refusal to take short cuts and to employ doubtful expedients, wins him the esteem of all who get to know him. His personal influence becomes a matter of much weight.

All this is argued from the standpoint of good policy. There is a higher standpoint, if we discuss the

35

question in the light of a man's duty to himself. What cause is so sacred that a man must lie for it? What gain is so great that one must warp his nature into that of a hypocrite in order to win it? Character is more important than great wealth; it is a poor exchange, for a man wilfully to transform himself into an habitual liar, a moral coward and a penurious epicure, in order to amass property.

Rather be just and fear not. Conduct regulated on that principle will not prevent prosperity. It will not destroy influence or esteem. It will, on the contrary, merit the approval of one's own conscience.

> "And more true joy Marcellus exiled feels,
> Than Cæsar with a Senate at his heels."

But Cæsar is extinguished more frequently than Marcellus is exiled.

The business man who is the soul of commercial honor, the incorruptible servant, the guileless clergyman and the mechanic, whose soul, through every vicissitude of fortune is still his own, are the types in demand. Whatever place they occupy—high or low—they are the models called for.

> "Tall men, sun crowned,
> Who live above the mob
> In public duty and in private thinking."

The Kernel of Progress. CAREFULLY study the influences of historical epochs, and the lesson they always teach in that progress has been the result of conviction. This is Emerson's meaning when he says that every revolution, however great, is at first a thought in the mind of a single man.

Peter, the Hermit, was possessed by the conviction that Christians should rescue the Holy Land from infidel rapacity. Other pilgrims had probably conceived the notion before the Hermit was born, but he alone let it sink into the depths of a purpose. How he became forthwith an incendiary of men's minds, and how from his impulse all Europe kept throwing itself against Asia for a period of two hundred years, is testimony in point, furnished by history.

The preacher of the Crusades may to one view seem a fanatic, but to all views his influence resulted in a stride forward for civilization. This is the inscrutable providence that rewards conviction. Commerce awoke, new lights shone, great discoveries were made, and when men reflected whence came this varied and simultaneous advance and progress, and whence dated the new spirit that animated it all, reference was at once made back to a preaching frair, traveling over the hills and valleys of Europe, uttering a conviction. There was the beginning, there was the man, and there was the thought that set the mass of men and events in motion.

These are the epochs we most like to dwell upon, because they present mankind, not as the play-thing of blind forces, but as an intelligence possessing moral purpose and free will. The pervasive growth of the anti-slavery movement in America is quite as creditable to this people as anything else in its history. At first the contention of a few earnest men whose petition to Congressman John Quincy Adams, ex-president though he was, jeopardized his political existence in presenting; their meetings were mobbed; their newspapers suppressed and themselves covered with ignominy and disgrace; yet by sheer force of truth and argument they found their way to the conscience of the country until they elected a president, who said: "This nation can not go on existing half-free and half-slave." And when the opportunity came, Abra-

ham Lincoln gave the blow which top-
pled over the slavery superstructure
forever. This was a triumph of principle from which, undoubtedly, has
ensued great industrial as well as great
moral good. No mere selfishness, however, could have induced the Garrisons
and the Phillips to labor as they did in
the face of an angry public. Selfishness would squat itself prone with
existing institutions. There would be
stagnation and inertia except for the
saving presence of a moral life in the
people, which breeds honest conviction
and impels a manly assertion of what
truth the conscience has to utter.

# THE COURAGE OF CONVICTION.

THE exigencies of modern times are such that men who wish to lead in thought can not sit on their opinions, or call in a jury of the vicinage to discuss mere proprieties. The wires are waiting and the press is ready for its food. Out with your opinion or your conviction while it is fresh and timely and while it has its use and its mission.

Men who are cravenly afraid of their own shadows neither cultivate their own respect nor the respect of others. They wait to see which way the cat jumps while braver men are prodding the feline in the right direction. Then, they are "ever strong upon the stronger side." It is a matter of fact, however, that such timorous souls make more mistakes of policy than even the outspoken, fearless man, who lets honest conviction be his sole guide and philosopher.

"Let any man once show the world that he feels
Afraid of its bark, and 'twill fly at his heels:
Let him fearlessly face it, 'twill leave him alone;
But 'twill fawn at his feet if he fling it a bone."

40

Of course there are occasions when
second sober thought will modify the
asperity of opinions and suggest the
wisdom of silence. But woe to the manliness of him who suppresses himself
too often or too habitually. Attrition
with the world of men and thought will
eventually cultivate a power of self-
discernment; and one will know whether the conviction that comes to him is a
matter of impulse or a matter of
principle.

Right
Rather
Than
Popularity.
IN democracies, strong men must,
now and again, refuse to bow to tempor-
ary waves of popular sentiment. They
must feel with Coriolanus in Shakespeare's play:

> "For the mutable, rank-scented many, let them
> Regard me, as I do not flatter, and
> Therein behold themselves."

In politics, a kind of leadership which
has no other policy than going with the
tide, cannot last because it cannot be
consistent. Next year the people may
go altogether contrary to the course
they have endorsed this year. The
majority pardons this fickleness in
itself, but it won't pardon it in a man
who claims to possess the capacity of

leadership. And the public is not slow to see a demonstration of moral courage in the action of a man who dares at times to be on the unpopular side.

**"Respectable" Opinions.** A SMOOTH path to prosperity is not the seeking of the best minds or the best men. This is particularly true as respects those who preach and teach and lead the community. What Horace Greeley says in one of his private letters is full of wholesome, good sense:

"No man knows better than I do that all the kingdoms of this world are to be acquired by just the opposite course from that I have chosen to pursue—by cottoning to whatever is established and popular, and warring upon novelties and innovations. I think I understand the philosophy of success as well as you do, and see why it is that 'the Son of Man had nowhere to lay His head' in an age and country which honored Herod, Pilate and Tiberius Cæsar. But I think I see that there is something better worth living for than temporal power, popularity and riches— that God's truth is still to be sought among the lowly, the despised, and the

outcast, and that whoso will serve God
and bless man must be esteemed exactly
as men of your stamp regarded Jesus of
Nazareth eighteen centuries ago, name-
ly, as a young man of rare abilities, high
courage, and blameless life, who might
do vast good if he would only abandon
his radical notions and low associations,
and conform to the orthodox creeds and
conservative instincts of his time. To
me the stable and the manger that sheltered the infant Saviour are not dead,
isolated records of what has been, but
the symbols of a truth that is vital and
impressive to-day."

The judgment of those who walk with
silk stockings on velvet carpets, who
live in a light toned and softened by the
arts of civilization and who breathe only
the intellectual perfume of the boudoir,
is not the thing for us to square ourselves with. When we cause it to fret
and exclaim, to hem and to haw at our
ungraciousness, to talk of "fanaticism"
and "imprudence," we have indications
of a negative character that we are
approximating what is right and just,
along the line of truth and courage, and
that we must not turn back or deflect.
The respectable and comfortable classes

in a republic like ours do not cherish the *summum bonum* of social and political development. They are what they are, largely per force of the ascendancy of their interests in the industries and legislation of the country. The real reformers may come, as they came in the time of Christ, from the fishermen of the nation—the lower stratum, not the higher; or from those who speak from and in behalf of these masses and keep in touch with them.

**Avant Couriers.** A GREAT writer has said that the truest patriots must always die as traitors — condemned by the unjust judgment of their times. We imagine that the age is becoming juster and more liberal to those who tell it unpleasant truths and herald radical ideas. Garrison and Phillips were frequently threatened by the "broad-cloth mobs" of Boston, but they lived to witness the success of the abolition movement. They died with the honors of liberators and not with the ignominy of traitors.

There are hundreds of men whose moral vision is clear enough, but who lack the stamina to declare themselves.

The task of the avant courier for a new movement or a pressing reform, is usually to supply courage as well as conviction. The movement frequently has to wait for the right crop of men as well as for the ripe opportunity.

Some of the conditions of modern society are decidedly adverse to the avant courier and his contention. We have a dull *juste milieu* of namby pamby compromises. To set one's face against the conformity required in the commercial, the political and the social world about us, requires a rarer courage than that which braved religious persecution in the past.

If one reads history with no other bias than a desire for truth, he is apt to reach the conclusion that conservatism has done more injury to mankind than even the wildest attempts at innovation and the crankiest of avant couriers. Courts have greater sins to answer for than revolutions, and some law-makers than some law-breakers. The conservative malevolence of Burke toward the French revolution is an illustration of the mistake of a standpoint. The results of that revolution outweigh

45

a hundred political philosophies like
that of the great Irish publicist.

> Once to every man and nation
> Comes the moment to decide.
> In the strife of truth and falsehood,
> For the good or evil side.
> Then it is the brave man chooses,
> And the coward stands aside
> Doubting in his abject spirit,
> Till his Lord is crucified.—*Lowell.*

**The Brave Man Chooses.** THERE is a choosing of this kind that
is not so heroic. It transpires almost
every day. Silence is golden then, in
the sense that it is convertible into
bankable funds.

Not once—but oftentimes, in every-
one's life there are moments to show
your colors. The constitutional coward
has a crabbed habit of shielding his own
miserable timidity by talking of the
"rashness" and temerity of braver men.
O'Connell was dubbed "a very rash
young man" by the older heads, when he
was leading the van for Catholic emancipation. "Unwise expressions"—"incendiary speeches"—these are the stock
phrases of men who are always waiting
and fanning themselves, but out of
whom the world or Truth never gets an
atom of good. There has never been

an assertion of great principles or of
salutary truths, from the Sermon on the
Mount to Magna Charta, from Magna
Charta to the Declaration of Independ-
ence, and from the Declaration of
Independence to the Proclamation of
Emancipation, that has not seemed
"unwisely rash" to—cowards.

Get Into Action. ONE of the new lessons that the first Napoleon added to the science of war was taught the Austrians in Italy. He showed them that they were too slow in coming into action. While they were wheeling their army about, he struck it in two places with the same French force. On the Austrian side there was lubberliness and procrastination; on the French side, energy, dispatch, celerity.

In a great fortification there is a big gun which, if loaded and properly pointed, will carry annihilation to any assaulting party. But when the fortification is actually assailed by an attacking party, those who man the walls find it necessary to overhaul the big gun, to readjust its position, to hunt about for its ammunition. The result is that the attacking party is upon the fortification before the big gun has come into action.

Now there are hundreds of men and women, both in the little and the big affairs of life, who are too slow in coming into action. They acquire an education, but fail to use it soon enough. They acquire wealth, but fail to enjoy it. They postpone the larger things of life with a sort of dilettant dilatoriness. They are like the people who are said to have an ambition to get into good society in Philadelphia: "it takes a lifetime to get in, and you get in only when you are ready to die." So these people realize that it is time to begin to live, only when they are about ready to die. They are "old men in a hurry"; rushing to catch the last train at the eleventh hour of their lives. And what is the matter? *They are too slow in coming into action.*

'To-morrow and to-morrow and to-morrow" MANY men see things as they are, and conceive things as they ought to be. But instead of action there is debate, indecision, temporizing, procrastinating, indolence and vacillation. Some wait for time which "heals all things." Some drift. Some console themselves with the thought that they must live in the world as they find it, and not as they would wish it to be.

We are not disparaging the grain of

practical philosophy to be found in each and all of these views. But a great deal remains undone, unchanged, unreformed, impenitent, bad, miserable and hell-bent, on account of this disposition.

With some, life is wasted in a vain forecast of

"To-morrow and to-morrow and to-morrow."

They put off achievements by which posterity might know them; worse than this, they put off virtuous living by which they might gain eternity. Their last to-morrow is an hour before death. And Lorenzo Dow has defined death-bed repentence to be burning out the candle of life in the service of the devil, and burning the snuff in the face of Heaven.

**Action is Power.** GENERAL SHERMAN found much wisdom in this passage which he quoted in an address delivered to the graduating class of a college in Michigan: "Of course knowledge is power, we all know that; but mere knowledge is not power; it is simply possibility. *Action* is power, and its highest manifestation is action with knowledge."

There must be action as we go along the pathway of life, if there is to be any power, or force, or mark in the career we are making. If one has convictions, let there be no time serving; now is the appointed time for their expression.

If a thing is right, the sooner it is done, the better. Whatever justice is due to me, I want it now. If there is anything good for me I must go directly and get it. If something needs reform, the speedier and more drastic the remedy, the better. If anything must be said, any understanding be had, any overhanging fate encountered, any change important, let these proper things begin forthwith.

If there is a good deed to be done, if there is a noble aim to be realized, if there are duties awaiting us in our daily lives, the time for all that is now before sunset.

"The flighty purpose ne'er is overtook
Unless the deed go with it; from this moment
The very firstlings of my heart
Shall be the firstlings of my hand."

# THE SOCIETY OF THE ENER-
## GETIC.

Daring
To Do. "THE society of the energetic class,"
Emerson tells us, "is full of courage, of
attempts which intimidate the pale
scholar." Animal spirits, daring and
robust energy, are absolute requirements
for him who would make his way in the
world. The bruiser succeeds often
when the scholar fails; all because he
has the sanguine grit, the elbow power
and push, depth of lung and swagger-
ing presence that command success.

Success is accidental with the timid.
But the bold carry the citadel of fortune
by sudden surprises. Timid people
pause upon the Rubicon of great
possibilities; the brave cast the die and
cross over. "You have greatly ventured,
but all must do so who would grandly
win."

The five great qualities of a good
commander, foresight, skill in the use
of resources, decision, dispatch and energy, are the qualities demanded, more

or less, of the good farmer and the good business man also.

The Discipline of Mind. MEN drift and dawdle, "tread the primrose path of dalliance," and so, halve the effectiveness and results of their lives. They do not talk to the point, but around it. They do not strike opportunities, but observe them. They diagnose evils and impediments, but they fail to take heroic measures. Tone and gesture indicate the habits of men in this respect. There is the ringing voice and the firm tread. Or the man ambles and shambles as he hems and haws.

The whole difference is due to self-culture. Colleges may, as Ingersoll says, "polish brickbats and dull diamonds." Station and opportunity may give us a thing and not a man. But the clear-cut character comes from sterling stuff within, working its will outwardly and forming the man according to an ideal that is bred in the bone and tingling in the nerves.

It is ever true in this matter that as a man sows so shall he reap. Let his mental habits encourage desultory thinking, and he dissipates his strength to perceive, reason and decide with precision. In trade and in the forum he will not know what he wants, and other men, keen-visioned for the main chance, will lead him.

Asleep to what is waking and stirring about him, he will lose his grip. Failing to cultivate all the activities by whose harmonious exercise the man of the world is brought into being, he will perpetually tread upon ground where he is unpracticed and unstrung.

The ever ready and ever decisive are neither shallow nor superficial, but self-cultured and self-controlled. They have submitted to discipline and austerity, where others have lived to no purpose.

"Self-knowledge, self-reverence, self-control,
These three alone lead on to sovereign power."

**Prescience.** As a rule, men strongly attached to causes and principles are apt to be impatient of events. Affairs move too slowly towards the consummation which they desire. Saws like "Rome was not built in a day," serve merely to irritate them.

Men of clear perception, however, may be strong partisans without being impatient. Their prescience calms their passions. They possess themselves thoroughly of the facts of the situation. Their vision sweeps the field. They are skilled in the arithmetic of forces. They put events together and see the conclusion in advance, just as the school boy grasps the inevitable circumstance of two and two making four.

When there is a great fact in history like a French Revolution, the careful historian, studying backward for the causes, marshals all the great tendencies that went directly to the making of the event. They are so clearly pictured forth, coming like giants with irresistible tread from the cavern of past years, that the reader may wonder why they were not discerned in their day—that they were not of public notoriety. Yet even the Cassandras of the time—who undoubtedly did prophecy what subsequently happened—had little faith in their own forebodings; they saw dimly what might occur if the world did not heed their homilies.

The culture of history and the training of affairs, social and political, combine to give men greater confidence in systems and tendencies than in isolated events and impulsive efforts.

**The Opportune Moment.** MEN of clear perception, who feel that their gift implies some moral obligation, may use it in many excellent ways. If wrong crushes over the field like a Juggernaut avalanche, these men know enough to stand out of the way and to husband their strength for the reaction, while evil is running its course. Or they may see the right moment of opportunity for sounding the alarm bell of a counter movement.

These opportune moments are the occasions for that exercise of clear vision, good judgment and steady nerve that give individuals their great use in history. When a thing is to be done, "he who dallies is a dastard, and he who doubts is damned." Makeshifts, patched-up truces are worse than useless.

Men who know what they want usually achieve something. Those who drift with the tide, shift with the wind, and take leaps in the dark, are the creatures, not the creators, of events.

Knowing what they want, knowing their resources, men of will and purpose have the decision, dispatch and energy that result in Acts. They are ready to take heroic measures.

What if they do cut through conventionalities? What if they overturn respectable Dignities and mild Peacemakers? The thing has to be done. The lance has to be applied. It is radicalism, but it is Cure. They burn their ships behind them, but there is an end to paltering counsels and temporizing methods.

Irresolution toys with opportunity. The loud demagogue vaunts it over subdued benches; the teachings of time-honored Bigotry and undisputed prejudices are proclaimed with haughty intolerance. Why shuffle and cower? Why not *bell the cat?*

Tallien hit the nail on the head when he defied Robespiere in the tribune, thus ending the Reign of Terror. O'Connell knew that he was precipitating the crisis of years when he decided to stand at the Clare election. He breathed a stranger courage into his millions of down-trodden, submissive countrymen. Up to his time they had been the abused and the villified. The pettiest magistrate claimed his title and his obeisance. Majesty and office expected them to cringe in the dust. O'Connell hurled epithets at majesty and office together, and gave the villi-penders of his race liberal measure of their own abuse in return. How like an electric thrill this boldness raised the spirit of a hunted race, let History speak!

The bloody Parisian mob, which made all the excess of the French Revolution possible, sought to renew the Reign of Terror, in Vandemaire, year four of the Revolutionary calendar. The mob, forty thousand strong, swarmed through all the streets of Paris towards the Convention Hall. It was the old plan to crowd in upon the Legislators and compel the issuance of sweeping, communistic, bloodthirsty decrees. This time the Convention employed a young artillery officer to defend it. His decisive preparatory moves settled the fate of the contest. He at once took the measures required by the situation; none but he, however, would have discerned with such swift intuition what was proper to the occasion. He ordered arms stored in one locality; posted guns in another street; threw up a barricade in a district that seemingly had no relation to the danger; stationed a reserve guard at an obscure church door, and so admirable was his provision that, when the Parisian mob appears in thousands for the onslaught, there is a whiff of grapeshot—"a very storm of shrieking cold lead." The mob scatters; the French Revolution is brought to a close, and the Age of Napoleon is born.

THE Spaniards have a proverb: "We will all be bald in a hundred years," intended, no doubt, to calm the nerves. For what are present losses and annoyances in the face of ultimate baldness? Why should we vex ourselves with petty disappointments; unnerve ourselves with the daily mishaps of business; grow sensitive over fancied slights; be consumed with jealousy or envy; hoard money; bother about influence, power or popularity?—a hundred years will see us stripped of everything,— even of our hair.

It was the happy conceit of an English writer to speak of a "tempest in a teapot." Tempests of this nature are only too common in the lives of everybody. Men fume and fret over matters of no consequence whatever. Half the nervous waste of the uproar would mend the mishap. The stew and sputter of yesterday will seem unaccountable to the calm reflection of to-morrow.

The habit induces its own excess. There is trouble enough as we go along in life without borrowing any. Yet some self-persecuted people are in perpetual bustle and furore; never content; always wanting more; grasping and covetous. Riches bring neither ease nor solace. They go on, making mountains out of mole-hills, and crossing bridges before they get to them.

The truth of the Spanish proverb will reach such persons in a much shorter time than a hundred years. "It is fret and worry and impatience and spasmodic fits of passion and anger which curtail our existence," says Dr. Hall. The poor live shorter lives than the rich, chiefly because the struggle for existence is harder with them. In France the average life of the wealthy man is twelve years longer than that of the laboring class.

Time cures everything. The lapse of hours and days smooths over the worst troubles. Griefs, seemingly the most poignant, are assuaged. Losses, the most irretrievable, are made up. Gulfs of estrangement are filled in. In the perspective of the past, trials furrowed on the memory lose all their magnitude.

"Blessed are the meek," it is said. And this is a benison upon serenity. The passionate, emotional and irritable are afflicted with the worst punishments. They cross their own purposes; dash every cup of genuine pleasure; cut the thread of their own lives, and live sweet in the memory of nobody. But the meek get to possess the land. The good things of life seem to be kept in store for them. Fortune likes the company of serenity. Religion, in deprecating worldliness, ought to have the effect of inclining its votaries to take things easy. "Be not solicitous concerning the affairs of this life." There is a system of compensation—an unvarying balance of good and evil. "No pain without its gain." Coolness and serenity ever enhance the pleasure and profit of living.

**Morbid Periods.** ONE does not have to follow altogether the lines of thought of Maudsley, respecting the influence of Body on Mind, to be persuaded that our moods and dispositions are largely determined by such matters as our diges-

tion and our physical condition generally.

We have our morbid periods—when
life seems dull and wholly uninterest-
ing or blank of any enjoyable prospect.
If we are prone to analysis, we separate
its complex structure into component
parts and ponder on the tawdry things
for which we seem to be living—wealth
and its creature comforts, friendships
that pass, and fame that blends into
the forgotten.

Now, in this frame of mind, the
right thing is to medicate the body. Get
out into the bracing atmosphere of a
winter's day. Try the experiment of
vigorous work. Walk away with brooding. Give wearied nature the soothing
treatment of a long sleep.

In these morbid states some people
say ill-tempered things, or write bad
prose and worse poetry, or come to unwise decisions. Play not on the guitar
when the instrument is out of tune.

The
Impolicy
of
Quarrels.

"THE meek shall possess the land."
That is the Biblical teaching. But the
contentious waste their energy in bitter
words and angry feelings. Half the

quarrels of life are avoidable. No man, looking back over the years, after the acrimony of some quarrel is allayed by time, but will admit to himself that it could have wisely been different.

Let us not deride the politicians in this respect. They nurse the good will of their neighbors. If there is a chance for collision with somebody they get around it or give "the soft word that turneth away wrath." It is always good politics and sometimes good Christianity to do as they do.

Every man has some merits. No man is wholly bad. Why should we nourish a feud with our fellow creatures, who are not much worse than are we ourselves, and who are perhaps no more to blame (for it takes two to make a quarrel). What principle is at stake, or is served, by two-thirds of the neighborhood clashes that gossips roll over their tongues? Analyze them and what do they disclose except the weakness of the contestants, their childish anger, or jealousy or envy, their choleric, stomachic or alcoholic folly, their want of fully developed, deepseated, keen-witted manliness, their inability to be philosophic enough to rise

above the pettiness and playthings of
life.

Some of us pride ourselves upon
coming of a fighting race. We take
conceit in our high spiritedness, our
ready gift of profane defiance, our
spunk and our impetuosity. Bah! It
is the courage of Falstaff, the temper
of the braggart. It is the cool, patient,
forbearing man in the long run who has
the most courage and the most principle. Your fighting race is good only
for its paid mercenaries, led by other
and cooler races. Your quarreling,
choleric, world-defying fellow accumu-
lates no results and wins no victories.

The
Art of
Persuasion. LOOKING at the world through colored glasses will not change the reality
of things. To hold definite views is
some evidence of a healthy and vigorous
mind. But to hold antipathies and
prejudices which ignore facts, is no better than to be altogether un-ideaed;
and sometimes it is worse.

The glow of passion only adds force
to one's views where there is the back-
ing of a peculiarly strong, well-in-
formed and logical mind. Many men
lose their power to make converts the

moment that their feelings are interested. They can talk better on the side opposed to their own convictions. There is a suggestion of this in the legal saying, that whoever acts as his own lawyer has a fool for a client.

It is advisable, in arguing your views, to dispense altogether with the motives of a partisan and have no wish whatever to persuade. "Gentlemen, these are the sad facts—see them or don't see them, but I will try to make them as clear as I can to you." Benjamin Franklin, whatever his shortcomings, must be conceded to have been a worldly wise man; and one of the first lessons he learned, in his attrition with men, was to state his views without heat or dogmatism. He "conceived" that such was or might be the case, or such was his "notion" or understanding. He pleased rather than antagonized, and, nevertheless, contrived to state his arguments as persuasively as any logic buffer.

We have altogether too much recrimination in place of evidence, and too much swash buckler, fish woman, jury-lawyer, penny-a-liner rhetoric, in lieu of gentlemanly common sense, spoken or written for an unbiased public.

# THE POINT OF VIEW.

The Poet's Eye. WHEN Robert Burns was plowing in the fields and uprooted a daisy, he stopped, and, full of tender sentiment, wrote a poem to the little flower. The ordinary plowboy would have gone on, without a single higher thought, in his drudgery.

Oh, for the eye and the heart of a poet in the lives we are living! Everything then has a deeper meaning, or a rarer beauty. The skies are bluer, the grass is greener, and the flowers speak a language that we understand. Why, there is all the difference in the world between what the poet gets out of life and what the dullard and grind see in it.

Now the poetic insight is not limited to those who write verses, for there are peasants who know not letters nor books, but who, looking out upon the beauties and sublimities of their mountains and valleys, have hearts filled with poetic fervor; and there is often a rude poetry in their spoken thoughts. Those who have no poetry in their souls, though they revel in wealth, are poorer than the peasants of Tyrol or Connemara; poorer in capacity of enjoyment.

There is another important sense, besides the poetic insight, that some men seem born without, or else it is lost by non-use, or stunted by the noxious growth of materialism and animalism. This other lost sense may be called the instinct of faith, or spirituality—the soul and the heart of one's nature. In the degree that a man's spirituality is developed so that his perspective reaches beyond this life, his heart losing none of the humanizing influences of the world and his years ripening and mellowing his sympathies, he is living a larger, a broader and a fuller life. If some other plowboy, working side by side with Burns on his Highland farm, had jeered at the poet when he picked up the daisy and made it the subject of a pathetic poem, it would hardly be fashionable for us to consider the plowboy the better man of the world. So when some over-fed physician, or mummified specialist, the major part of whose nature lies crushed

under his materialistic pursuits, fails to
appreciate the message of the great
preacher, or the spiritual life and
insight that actuates Christian men and
women, there should, similarly, be little
question of the attitude of liberally
educated men. Those who lack the
spiritual sense are as deficient as those
who lack the poetic sense.

The
Habit of    To cultivate a habit of always seeing
Satire. the awkward or ridiculous aspect of
things is unwise. Cynical remarks can
be passed respecting all men and all
happenings. Life is nothing but dregs
and lees to one who educates himself
out of the possibility of admiring,
praising or wondering. It is a mourn-
ful routine with the man whose blood
does not sometimes boil with honest
indignation. If the habitual sneer is
not occasionally chased away by a
square smile or a broad grin, then life
is sad, indeed. If you are settled down
in a rut of insipid bitterness, with no
vision of the good, the true or the beautiful, it is time to travel. Go to the
world's cataract at Niagara and see if
your eye will not brighten at the

stupendous master stroke of nature there exhibited. Stand in the presence of heroism and test whether your jaded nerves will not thrill and tingle with admiration. Visit the great gala occasions of nations when all that is grand and imposing in the resources of power, wealth and splendor is displayed, and try if you cannot observe and wonder.

The habitual satirist tears down, but never builds up. He spins no meshes of thought which bind facts into a fabric of useful and helpful experience. His words are disparagement, chill and discouragement. Effort palls, hopes die and purposes wane under the jaundiced notice that he takes.

Say a good word. Utter a timely suggestion. Bestow praise where it will bias to the right. Cheer honest effort. Overlook the flaws, and let the main aspect alone attract your attention. Then the path of your influence will be marked by certain results; where, with the habit of satire, your path would be strewn with wrecks and abandoned efforts, begun in faith and deserted in cynicism.

Shapes of Vice.

THE lawyer in the Scriptural tale, who asked the Son of God what he must do to be saved, was substantially informed that by loving God and his neighbor he might thereby keep all the commandments. This method of summarizing the virtues in one broad act of charity cannot be safely pursued with reference to the vices. There are, according to the moralists, seven deadly sins—all bad and all distinct; and they have existed in their individualities from the beginning, working themserves out in various malignant originalities of their own.

It does happen that some of the vices are more dangerous to special persons and classes of persons than to others. Lust may be the predominant fault of one nationality, while avarice is that of another. And certain vocations may be more exposed to one kind of transgression than to another. Or, because of the voluntary practice of some exalted virtue, like chastity or obedience, the opposite vice may become the chief of the sins to struggle against.

As an obvious consequence, one's state of life has a good deal to do with the way in which he views the vices.

A clergyman speaking at an impressive convent ceremony where some young ladies had taken the veil, said:

"Unchastity is the great sin—I may say, the only sin. An unchaste man is the most horrid object the pure stars look down on. Without chastity, domestic life, social relations, and peace on earth are impossible. Turn lechery loose upon the world and a devouring flame of hell will roll over the world, leaving only blackness and death behind."

To the view of those who have adopted the religious state of life this undoubtedly is no exaggeration. And to any vocation, whether worldly or unworldly, unchastity cannot be depicted in colors too abhorrent or revolting.

Yet there are others of the vices which to the great majority of mankind, are probably more dangerous. Even as respects the religious state, the old legend will occur to the reader: The monk was given his choice to commit one of three sins. He chose drunkenness as the least abhorrent. He became intoxicated and committed the other two sins.

The story is probably one of those moral fables which spring from a capacity for vivid illustrations, but who cannot discern its "truth to life"? What Herbert Spencer calls the "theological bias" in the intellectual life, may, also, have some existence in moral matters. The monk, probably, showed in his exhortations that he thought gluttony less of a deadly sin than he deemed unchastity. It was the cult and bias of his high and unworldly vocation, and nothing more.

**Not All One Way.** THE Duchess of Argyle wrote to Charles Sumner: "Do you remember that you never can be engaged in a cause again where right and wrong stand face to face as they did in the anti-slavery fight? In most human struggles, they are much mixed together."

Charles Sumner did not heed this advice. He went into the new political contests that followed the war as if they were Homeric battles — all the good on one side and all the evil on the other. The result was that he got out of joint with "practical politics" and in 1872 his own party—wherein he had been a great leader—was obliged to unhorse him.

In theological contests, good men are always fighting the Devil. When they fall out among themselves the mode of warfare is not readjusted. They fight each other as if the devil were still in the contest. Probably he is; but there is some of him on both sides. And there is a modicum of good on both sides.

**The Wisdom of our Elders.** OFTEN the sage counsel of those who have lived out the essential facts of life seems to the quick pulsations of youth too narrow—too prudent—too cold. Men and women, grandsires and grand-dames, who have had all the experience of births, marriages and deaths, take habitually a safe, a conservative, a calculating view of the questions that come up in careers.

With them there should be little venture and no adventure. It is steady go —and slow. "Out of the beaten tracks thy fathers trod, thou shalt not depart." Our elders are ever passing a vote of want of confidence in youth, not

because they disparage it, but because
of their kindness for it. The babe
needs protection. No matter how man-
like her son may grow, his mother never
feels he can bear what his father has
borne. Those of our elders who have
gone through a life of hardship and
arrived at some comfort in their old
age, are inclined to make the question
of bread and butter and shelter an
unduly large consideration in life.

Observe how it operates in their
views of marriage. The novels and
plays for centuries are based on collis-
ions between the prudence of her
father and the romance of his daughter.
Men have been selecting their wives for
generations, more upon the color of the
hair, the light of an eye or the round-
ness of a dimple, than upon the
question of dowry.

After all, is the wisdom of our elders
so very wise, that the world has been
diluting it so much in actual life
with the illusions, romances and
impulses of youth? Possibly we might
all be better; but, possibly, too, we
should grow sadder as we grew wiser.

Narrow-
Guage
Statesmen. THE councils of state have always been troubled by the political old fogy —narrow viewed and narrow guaged— with his exaggerated fear of "entangling alliances," his parsimony of economy and his quibbling views of the limitations of the constitution.

Jefferson was a strict constructionist; yet, when the time came to perform a brilliant act of statesmanship, he "strained the constitution until it cracked"—(to use his own words), and bought Louisiana, out of which a dozen states have since been "carved." Monroe was a man of the utmost prudence, but his Monroe doctrine, put forth just in the nick of time, was the boldest blast of American Republicanism that reactionary Europe ever heard. Adams, with his plea for "lighthouses in the sky," and Clay with his Panama congress, intended to knit the sister republics of the western hemisphere into a closer commercial unity, were leaders in a broad kind of statesmanship that properly characterized a youthful, vigorous and Titanic nation. Every stroke of such men, from the purchase of Louisiana, the acquisition of Florida, the conquest of Texas and the buying of Alaska, has paid the nation manifold, and to omit them would have been palpable and stupendous folly.

Yet then and now and evermore like measures will be attacked by finical persons in the pose of conservative statesmen, whose views are as broad as their "district," or whose bucolic prudence or *blasé* indolence is offered as a safe and worthy spirit for the nation.

When Blaine proposed his peace congress of the western republics, these owlish conservatives of the country's safety set up a prolonged objurgation against such jingoism. When there is further talk of acquiring Canada or of constructing a system of coast defences, the same narrow spirit is encountered. Not every innovation is a reform, and not every new prospect is either safe or desirable. Nevertheless, good things there are, and many of them, waiting the adoption that a great republic like this can give them, to return us benefits

manifold. But the cross-road states-
man looms athwart them with his dis-
tressing discretion, and the nation is
held to the range of an intellect that
could feel roomy in the emoluments of
a village squire.

Radicalism.  ALL good causes need the spice of
radicalism. Your evenly balanced,
judicious and careful movements suffer
from apathy and want of enthusiasm.
Talk with spirit, argue with aggres-
siveness, take advanced grounds and the
crowd will come to listen.

Perhaps they will not all agree with
the extreme position taken. But he
who leads must always be in advance.
The multitude will never get but half
way, and if the agitator stops at half-
way compromises and "golden means"
the multitude will not budge farther
than a quarter the distance.

Then, there is a contagious pleasure
in carrying propositions to their logical terminus. The conservative stops
with the goody goody; the radical wants
the whole truth, and nothing but the
truth.

Young men are radicals by constitution. No movement that has not in it something of the courage, the dash and the audacity of radicalism, can win their hearty adherance. Grant that they attempt too much, or, hope too extravagantly; it will be time enough for them to turn conservatives when they grow old.

We must not be too ready to propose compromises before the opposing side arrive at a tractable spirit. And there is no better way to force a tractable disposition upon our opponents than by carrying our contention to its ultimate sequences. There is a certain unreasonableness in radicalism that makes the stubborn evil, which it antagonizes, glad to be reasonable and willing to treat upon any fair basis. This circumstance is apparent in all history: in the granting of power to the people; in the destruction of feudalism; in the downfall of slavery; and in the decline of landlordism.

Time for the Puritan. PURITANISM is a social medicine—unpleasant to take, obnoxious as a steady diet, but often, when taken—good medicine.

Ordinary Christian ministration does little or nothing to affect the social evil —that canker of city life that among Christians should not be as much as mentioned. Ordinary Christian ministration has an apparent truce with saloonism—an institution, in its American form, rotten to the core and branded with the mark of hell.

But aroused Puritanism—especially masculine Puritanism—makes headway against these evils; and it is the only thing that does make headway. Why should we not have mobs on the side of morality? The wrath of God, speaking in the voice of an aroused people, is the only thing under the new dispensation that will bring fear into the haunts of sin. If there is any better way to fight the devil than with fire, experience has not taught it. As toward a great evil—the money lenders in the temple—there were no persuasive pleadings; it was the lash and the scourge, summarily, right and left, until the evil was cleaned out.

This is the only method with the evils that afflict the morality of our cities. We are living now under a truce with the devil. The intelligence, morality and respectability of our large cities, regarded as a force (and aside from individual exceptions) stand secluded from the lower stratum, yet not unaffected by it; for they feed it with fresh recruits, the punishment for not fighting it.

The times are ripe for the Puritan to appear. Good people, we may shrink back from his raining of fire and brimstone. But do not sneer at him—earnestness is always respectable. We may live when he is buried under popular odium to enjoy his clean Sunday and to get the benefit of the strong moral force he has infused into public opinion.

A Lesson in Public Spirit. IN times of war, when men volunteer in defense of our common country, we admire their patriotism and commend their public spirit.

Peace hath its duties no less important than war. If it be meritorious to risk one's life to defend the nation, it is also meritorious to devote one's time and attention to elevate and improve the nation.

The bravery that we all admire in the

soldier is also manifest by the citizen who volunteers his aid and presence to all public spirited movements.

In 1862 many Americans who had profited by the liberty and security given them by a free government, left the endangered Union and sheltered themselves in Canada until the trouble was all over.

Hundreds of us are doing similarly mean things to-day. We see movements afoot for the betterment of our fellow-men and we never lend a hand. We miser our time and our sympathy. We "let others do it"; fearing that we will lose something if we participate, or that we will be mussed up in the jostle, or have our respectability impaired.

Want of public spirit is to be looked upon as a defect in character—a sort of deficiency in capacity for friendship and sympathy.

We all owe something to our community and in paying such indebtedness we earn for ourselves a rounder life and a fuller citizenship. These duties to the community may be different for different individuals. One may hold office, another may found an art gallery, still another may visit the sick.

But no man should be without some method of exercising his public spirit. He will find his duty not far away and it may be simple and unostentatious.

Now and then a young man sighs for the pomp and circumstance of war, that he may show his heroism. He would carry his country's flag in the face of the foe and plant it on the ramparts of rebellion. But in the life about him he is too apathetic to attend a caucus or assist in some parish good work. Have we here the makings of a hero or of a braggart? A man who requires the exceptional circumstance of war to show his public spirit is too luxurious a subject for the modern state. These are times when the arts of peace are most useful; and a citizenship which has its fruition in the good works of civil life is the citizenship we want. As Milton said:

"Peace hath her victories
No less renowned than war."

THERE are hundreds of men who sell their votes for a consideration — a thousand dollars, a five dollar bill, a glass of beer. In the aggregate, these men sell their country. A time may come when supreme national interests depend upon the results of a close election. And the contest will go against the country because some men take money for their votes.

"Thank God, I have a country to sell," said O'Grady, member of the Irish Parliament that passed the Act of Union. O'Grady was a practical man and had realized several thousand pounds for his vote. Was he going to allow a mere matter of sentiment to interfere with a profitable deal?

It is only a sentiment that actuates an honest man in rejecting a bribe for his vote. But after all, money is not everything in this life. Every man's experience testifies to that. There are values beyond the ratings of dollars and cents. Chastity in a man or woman is only a sentiment, perhaps. Brutalize and materialize society to a certain point, and that will be its view of the case. That is no argument, however, against the value of a sentiment. Patriotism itself is a sentiment. So is that "sensibility of principle" and that "chastity of honor" which feels a stain like a wound. Milton praises

> "that good earl, once president
> Of England's council and her treasury,
> Who lived in both unstained with gold or fee,
> And left then both, more in himself content."

A long and honorable public career may be a matter of sentiment. A sterling sense of honor in private life may be a matter of sentiment. But there isn't money or property enough in the world, there isn't gold enough coined, plated, lost, buried or undug to buy a tenth part of these mere sentiments at the value those who cherish them, hold them, and at the appreciation we are glad to believe the public still puts upon them.

THE impressive feature, in the statuary of the Greeks, was power in repose. It is thus in all art, and it is thus in the part every man plays in life. In painting, poetry and oratory, the pleasing feature is the sense imparted of a possible higher flight, a fullness of power beyond—not put forth, but held in reserve. The great orator sways by his evident mastery over the deep feeling that possesses him, allowing it to break forth only now and then in a glow of passion, studied, controlled and dominated by reason; giving the impression that, thrilling as his periods are, he has thunder in reserve, that he is doing with ease what he might far excel did he but let himself out. This apparent ease of execution is the gracefulness of art; for grace must have the quality of easiness, just as beauty gains by seeming unconscious of itself.

Now, in life there is wisdom in the Biblical counsel: "Let your self-restraint appear to all." The forgiving spirit seems the type of finest nobility of character, because it implies so much restraint. Patience, abstinence, courage, modesty and all the higher virtues partake of this quality.

One's Own Individuality. EXPERTS, in cases of forgery, testify that it is one chance in many hundreds of thousands that a man ever signs his name thrice in exactly the same manner. If the similarity occurs, it is generally true that microscopic investigation will discover pencil tracings which will demonstrate the forgery.

Though coming from the hand of the same Maker, no two men are ever alike. Every creature has his individuality, his characteristic way and peculiar manner, which, out of all the things of the universe, he may most truthfully call his own. This individuality should be cherished and not cheapened, because somewhere close to it lies the man's true worth and sincerity. If he has self-respect he will not hide his individuality. It will appear in all his actions. Men will feel that nobody else but he would have thought this or said that; nobody else but he would have done the job in just the way it has been done, or acted thus under similar circumstances.

It is to be noted that this individuality permits us to separate its possessor from the monotonous many. It is to his life and the impress that he makes upon society something like a name or a designation. So if men wish to be known for their usefulness, they must develop those talents and aptitudes that they possess in the highest degree, and just in proportion as this is done will they have lived to a purpose. The crowd of servile imitators who never call their own individuality into play, live lives of inanity. But whether peasant, poet or politician, the man who is truest to his own instincts gives the world the most forceful service.

Signs of Character.

MORAL courage is sometimes referred to as "character." It indicates strength of will, and a right appreciation of principle. When little men are bending to the whirlwind of excitement or succumbing to pressure, this man acts right in the face of prejudice or of his own advantage, and all men in their secret souls admire his course.

There are men who carry this method of action with them, as a kind of second nature, in all the affairs of life. They instinctively do right. There is no circuity or timeserving in their way of dealing with men and subjects. They establish a knowledge of their conduct in this respect among their neighbors, and it stands for their character.

But manners are also taken as indicative of character. Men are loud, self-assertive and pushing. They grasp, crowd and over-reach. Other men are constitutionally timid. They do nothing bold or bad because they have no taste for it. They have the quiet, subdued bearing of gentlemen, but it is not so much the repose of character as the imbecility which comes from want of character.

Where conscious power and able energy are quiet and unassuming, as when the "observed of all observers" places himself rather in the back ground; when merit takes the lowest seat at the banquet table; when there is every appearance of self-abnegation and unselfish attention to the wants and pleasure of others, we certainly have the manners of a gentleman. And it is not unusual to take it for granted that such conduct is predicated upon a fine character, upon right sympathies and broad views.

Still another direction in which a sign of character is often perceived is in one's likes and dislikes. A man who is faithful to his friends and hateful to his enemies is said to evince character. He is a worker in either case. There is nothing flabby or clammy about him. When he fights you will know that he is throwing his whole weight into the contest, and that he will go down with his flag flying, or hammer his way to victory. It is the militant disposition which is made of sterling stuff—for fighting. The Templar in Ivanhoe is an illustration. But, after all, was he a good man? Other elements may be lacking.

Goodness is taken as a frequent index of character. Austerity and piety denote a proper contempt for worldliness and a certain strength of will. The saint is thoroughly in earnest. He has a serious conception of life. If well-defined views of man's mission, grown into deep convictions decisively influencing every action and modifying the whole course of one's life, count for anything, then the good man doubtless possesses character.

# RECURRENCES.

THERE are times when old causes become wearisome. The gamut of argument is exhausted. There is nothing more to be said. Advocacy runs into reiteration. The public is tired. It craves peace. It wishes the subject changed. Admitted that the cause is good; that the world needs conversion to it; that ceaseless agitation seems to be the only means. Yet the sympathetic public mind is like the farmer's soil. It wants a rotation of crops. It wants to follow the good old Biblical rule—to lie fallow for a while, so that its nerves may regain their normal condition, and its emotions may be calmed and solaced.

This is the reason that the world eagerly turns to new causes—when they are opportunely broached. Presented at the high tide of some thoroughly earnest movement, they wait for attention; but in the ebb tide they quickly attract notice, repute and adherence.

The world of thought and action does not rotate about one center. There are various circles engaging men's minds and sympathies and energies. While the moral world is troubled by one movement, a separate and distinct movement may be widening out in the political sea. Of course, these circles cut into each other and absorb each other. And all have their counterparts and consequences. After a movement has practically disappeared in the moral world, it may reappear in the world of politics. The Quaker sect was agitated with an anti-slavery movement nearly a half century before the storm burst with decided force upon the political sea.

Side by side with an anti-divorce movement in morals may proceed a civil service reform in politics, an industrial training movement in education, and an eight-hour agitation in the economic world. None of these movements may be strong enough, deep enough or permanent enough to widen out from morals into politics, or from education into morals. But this sometimes does happen when the world is thoroughly in earnest. The slavery agitation swept every chord, political, social, moral and literary.

In the domain of human rights, and in the moral world there is really nothing new or unfamiliar. There would seem to be no room here for new causes. And yet new causes are perpetually arising. They have all the indications of novelty. They have new applications to begin with. There are new ears open to them. They choose new names, new watchwords, new leaders and new fields.

Analyzed with accuracy, however, these supposed "new causes" are really old contentions and old movements rehabilitated. Deep down, are the same principles. They rest on the same foundations. We can recognize in them affairs that have been before the world in former years. Daniel Webster made speeches for civil service reform in the '30's. Jesuit Fathers taught manual training to an extinct civilization in Paraguay two hundred years ago. Wat Tyler was the predecessor of the Knights of Labor, and there were mediæval prototypes of prohibition. The crinoline of 1886 was a rëappearance of that of 1865.

This phenomenon is symptomatic of the public desire for change and variety. If there is right and truth behind a movement, we can never be sure that its present disappearance is any evidence that it is permanently dead. It is merely permitting the public to take a rest. It will burst in upon the world later on in a new form, with new energy. The fittest survive. Weak and fanciful ideas have no second birth, but right and truth enjoy an eternal renascence.

"Paramount Rights." IT is alleged that one of the deep questions over which some mediæval school-men cudgeled their erudite brains was: "How many angels can dance on a needle point?" Did they ever find out? Not that we know of; and the problem is really not worth a journey to heaven.

Questions of this kind will settle themselves eventually. Perhaps the cowled school-men ascertained with mathematical nicety the answer to their problem the day after they touched the green sward of the other world.

So the future will answer for us many

of the questions of "paramount rights" that we now somewhat fruitlessly discuss. The mutual rights of the Church and State was another Middle Age question over which men-at-arms as well as schoolmen perturbed themselves. It was the issue between the Popes and the Emperors: Kingcraft *versus* priestcraft—the canonists *versus* the hired lawyers of the monarch.

This question is in process of most agreeable settlement in these, our days. Between the Church and the State there is towering up the Individual both in his Personal and his Family Relations. It is he who is umpiring the old game once bloodily fought out between Guelph and Ghibelline.

The Individual is putting limitations upon the State that the Popes long ago craved for. Our Constitutions are mainly (especially in their Bills of Rights) limitations upon State power—so many "Thou shalt nots" that the majority and the Legislature must obey. The Individual also has upon his side the spirit of the age and the tendency of the times. There is Jeffersonian Democracy arguing that the least government is the best government—that the State should not only keep off the grounds that the Constitution prohibits it from entering, but that it shall also, through motives of expediency, public policy, liberty and popular character, keep off other grounds as well. The Great Voluntary Agencies to which modern society has given birth, such as the press, the school, the private association and the Church, are excellently performing much of the work that the State formerly bungled and blundered at.

The canonists may feel relieved from laying down with precision what the State "must" and "must not" do. Suarez was far in advance of his age. But we are catching up to the "known laws of ancient liberty." Those who speak of the Church asserting paramount rights over the State, or those who think it necessary for the Church to lay down the limits of State power, are really listening to echoes of a conflict whose turmoil is four hundred years back.

**Lost Arts.** SOMEBODY, who wants to interest the public, might find a mine of entertainment in looking after "the lost arts." The stained glass of the middle ages and the wonderful "Greek fire" spoken of in the description of sieges and naval fights, are topics of live interest to this inventive age. Can we rediscover this lost knowledge of man? Can we revive the erudition of the Alexandrian library or resurrect the Rabbinical lore of the Jews?

Perhaps we can. But there are other lost arts, too. Chivalry is one of them. Faith is said to be another. But neither faith nor chivalry is wholly lost. We are simply deprived of the mediæval article. It comprised qualities which would greatly enrich the faith and courtesy of the modern world. To this extent faith is a lost art. The saints and the miracles of other ages seem no longer to favor this age. But this may be due to a failure to see the good lives that are being led and a failure to appreciate the great wonders that are transpiring. The French infidel who said that he would not go to see the Ascension of Christ, even if that event should reoccur in the Paris of the nineteenth century, typifies a species of unbelief that is current. Such men follow the agnostic in declaring that "they thank God that they are atheists."


**Reverence.** NOR has the estimable quality of reverence departed from the modern world. There is as much of it as ever; only it is differently distributed. We still admire and esteem greatness, goodness, purity and worth-in-position.

The world of other days reverenced a king, apart from his character. The modern world reverences a good king but despises a bad king. That is the difference. We do not altogether think of the place or the function; we think also of the man who fills it and the character he bears. This disposition to make reverence a matter of reason improves the quality of the reverence as well as the breed of kings. We are obtaining a better class of kings than those of other centuries. If the king is not nature's nobleman—a gentleman —we do not care to number him among our acquaintances. But if his character is exalted as well as his station, and his life as pure as his function is grand, then there is more reverence in our quiet esteem and confidence in him than in all the obsequious bowings and plaudits of a half superstitious and half-ignorant multitude.

Reverence departed? Not at all. It is only those, who in high station have failed to deserve reverence, that fancy the modern world has no reverence. 'Tis a way they have of flattering themselves. If reverence were given out of mere respect for place and function it would be no better than a time-server and a parasite. I think more of the friendship and manliness of him who gives to an ordinary baronet high esteem that he would never give to a mean king, than I do of the hypocrite who pretends to honor the miserable king out of respect to his office but deliberately forgets the worthy baronet's name.

# THE KNOWLEDGE OF EVIL.

A Question of Innocence. "A RED cheeked peach that does not know anything but the dew and the sun, and to grow sweet and pretty—it goes wrong when it is wrenched off the stem and eaten by a hog," which, paraphrased in a newspaper article, reads this way:

"A rosy cheeked girl who does not know anything but a mother's love and a father's love, and day by day grows sweet and pretty—she goes wrong when she is torn away from home and thrown where the temptations and pitfalls of vice are about her."

We do not like to believe that innocence—trustfulness in the goodness of human nature, is a source of weakness amid the struggles of life in a great city. Must we educate against this innocence in order to protect the pathway of the virtuous?

In any event, it is a safe and practical step for men and women of goodwill, everywhere to oppose all things that may deceive innocence, and to do away, even by force and violence if necessary, with the pitfalls that ensnare the unwary. Christian civilization should mean a state of society, in which innocence may live unscathed, and unendangered; and purity, may go about without guardianship, much as the lady in the Irish ballad:

"Rich and rare were the gems she wore,
 And a bright gold ring on her wand she bore
 But oh! her beauty was far beyond
 Her sparkling gems or snow white wand."

"Lady! dost thou not fear to stray
 So lone and lovely through this bleak way?
 Are Erin's sons so good or so cold
 As not to be tempted by woman or gold?"

"Sir Knight! I feel not the least alarm,
 No son of Erin will offer me harm—
 For though they love women and golden store,
 Sir Knight! they love honor and virtue more."

**An Apostolic Caution.** ST. PAUL said, "Let not such things even be mentioned among Christians" —or words to that effect.

And yet St. Paul went in for the purification of society. He was a preacher of the highest morality to an age when the Roman world was being undermined by voluptuousness and indulgence. If ever a preacher had material and provocation to paint the evils

102

in society with a teeming sensational-
ism, the opportunity was St. Paul's.

He did not do it. He refrained. The
advertisement of corruption in all the
red lights of rhetoric, with a little moral appended and "thou shalt not,"—was
not his method. People do not need to
have evil described to them in order to
avoid it. The knowledge of evil may
be a temptation to evil. The fewer
"If Christ Came to Chicago" books that
go from the press the better. The fewer
exploitations of "Maiden Tributes,"
issued in behalf of good morals, the better for good morals.

**Degenerate
Tendencies.** It has been somewhere remarked—
and with no little truth—that it is the
*monotony* of good and the *variety* of
evil that accounts for the sins of the
average man. Naturally he prefers
well-doing. His reason strongly ap-
proves right living and, in his remorse,
condemns any deviation from correct
principles. But goodness is monotonous—evil, if it is all known, gets to be
attractive as a break in the hum-drum
of regularity and virtue.

So, very often, as a kind of relaxa-
tion, otherwise sensible men have "made

103

a night of it;" gone on a wild carousal, breaking all their rules of rectitude, virtue and honor. Their cool reason informs them that, leaving moral considerations wholly out of the question, there is no pleasure whatever in the "good time" that is had in debauchery and late hours. The taste for variety is, to their cooler second thought, the only explanation for a proceeding that they strongly condemn when it is over.

Now, it is just possible that there is something wrong in a life of regularity which has a craving for the variety of sin. A wholesome method and condition of living has its satisfactions within the moral code. It has no erotic, erratic or abnormal promptings. There is incipient disease somewhere, if there is an overdose of temptation to be resisted. We are not all to be tried as St. Anthony was in the desert. We are flattering ourselves if we think so. Such exhibitions of moral fortitude are given only great saints. Ordinary mortals, in a normal condition of living, are providentially exempted from too much of the devil.

In our goody-goody hum-drum dog-trot method of living, we are to inquire for the seeds of moral disease before waiting to be laid up on the sick bed of sin. People take long journeys for their physical health or change their business to avoid bodily mishaps. It may be that similar upliftings from a rut are needful to the moral welfare of man. He may need adversity to put him on his mettle; responsibility to give him aim and purpose; change of location to get away from depressing or degrading associations. Let people of good reputation who crave at times the variety of evil, look to their moral hygiene. There is something bad about their goodness,—that is all.

**The Black Art.** THE poor old devil is having a hard time with this modern agnostic community. People won't believe in him. He gives evidence enough of his existence, it is true, in this bad, wicked world. Read the news dispatches of Monday, recording the devilment of the preceding day!

That is the "black art" that we are exclaiming against. It matters little what superstitious people may say or believe about men being "possessed by the devil," or obtaining diabolical powers to do mischief. It matters little what skeptical people may say or believe about Satan not having power to actually manifest himself in the flesh.

We see enough of his "black art" in the misery and crime cropping out in our large cities. It is not natural that men should be so bad as to do these inhuman, revolting things. We say, it is the devil and his black art. The trail of the serpent is over it all. Mephistopheles is flitting around these dark places. Beelzebub is there. Satan is present. The witches are there, three times three, and three fold, with their devilish incantation about their bubbling caldron, brewing evil for mankind.

"Double, double, toil and trouble."

We good people have so much to do getting rid of such material devilment that we can discover all about us (and sometimes within us) that we have no time to be led away, as the old Puritan Fathers at Salem were, with will-o'-the-wisp fancies about sorcerers and spirit rappers. For our part, we are willing to give all the witches in Christendom free scope to jump their brooms in the clouds, if they will only catch up all the bad bartenders by the slack of the trousers and carry them off.

TRUTH is unchangeable, but we ourselves change in our relation to truth.
We come, year by year, to grasp it more
fully and with great perfection; or by
a series of mischances we drift away
from its purity and completeness.

Sir Isaac Newton, in the closing
years of his life, said: "I do not know
what I may appear to the world, but to
myself I seem only like a boy playing
upon the seashore, and diverting myself
by now and then finding a pebble or a
greater shell than ordinary, while the
great ocean of truth lies all undiscov-
ered before me."

Man in his higher development is a
progressive revelation unto himself.
Emerson says:

"Out from the heart of Nature rolled
The burden of the Bible old,
The litanies of the nations came
Like the volcano's tongue of flame,
Up from the burning core below,
The canticles of love and woe."

Truth is in the Universe and in
human intelligence, but Time and

struggle and events are necessary to develop it. "The laws of nature are the thoughts of God."

New epochs are new testaments. The Emancipation Proclamation, for instance, is a chapter (taken in connection with the events that led up to it) worthy of a place in any Bible. Every reform is a new dispensation, so far as it goes, and every reformer is a prophet or a sage.

The volume of God's truth is too vast, and the process of its revelation too gradual, to make it possible for Moses or the procession of secretaries to human progress who followed him, to set it down within a single book. The idea of making the Bible a limitation upon one's beliefs appears narrow compared to the broader teaching, which makes the Church a supreme court, ruling over and collating a body of truth and revelation that books do not contain and that Time is still making clearer and fuller.

**Hush! Hush!** WHATEVER leads to better living: whatever conduces to higher thinking: whatever inculcates principles of honor, virtue and honesty—all this is religion.

But controversies have arisen and harsh things are said in defense of good teachings; and tranquil-minded people find this unpleasant. They want a religion of perpetual peace. They will find it, alas! nowhere on this side of the grave.

Struggle seems to be a condition of life; and in every department of it— spiritual as well as material. If we read the lives of some of the greatest saints, we shall find that they were temptation-tossed and tribulation-driven, too. Doubts and anxieties and jealousies crossed their minds and they found need for all the grace that prayer and good works and the sacraments could impart.

It is, possibly, indifferentism and worldliness in religion that craves so strongly for peace and quietude. Religious questions trouble the votary of pleasure and overtax the strength of the weakened spiritual nature. The idea of religious peace which comes about crying "hush," "hush," is not a Christian idea. Controversies will arise and men will go at religious issues with the imperfection of the human side showing

out most prominently. There will be
stormy times in the council. Even
scandals may arise, but all this, while
regretable, is much better than drift-
ing down the placid waters of indifferentism to the broad bay of doubt and
disbelief.

**In God's Time.** THE Almighty who made the world
and with Whom resides the power to
unmake it is reigning over it. In His
own good time He will bring about the
changes and reforms that seem desirable. In the contemplation of His wisdom our impatience should be silent.

But possibly we are His instruments
for the bringing about of those changes
and reforms that seem desirable? In
that case our concern is not in the
smooth sailing nor the success of the
movement in which we engage, but in
the fullness with which we do our duty
as we see it. "Act well your part—
there all the honor lies." And therein
all our responsibility is discharged.
God's purposes are not necessarily
furthered by our personal victories: our
defeats and failures may pave the way
to the end we have labored for with-

out apparent results. Martyrdom is defeat; and yet in the history of religion and liberty, and progress, martyrdoms have frequently presaged and prepared the way for abiding success.

"Think Ye?" "THINK ye that those upon whom the tower of Siloam fell were sinners above all those who dwelt in Jerusalem?"

A Biblical text for the consideration of the thoughtful. Doubtless there were more responsible people in Jerusalem upon whom the tower of Siloam might as properly have fallen; but they escaped.

That tower of Siloam has been tumbling every generation since the prophets walked in Judea. The question may be repeated here and now with equal pertinence:

Are not we, who fail to create a strong public opinion against social and industrial evil, sinners in every modern Jerusalem? And might not the tower of Siloam, in the shape of famine or pestilence, or fire or social obloquy, or financial crash, fall upon us to crush us for apathy and indifference?

It does sometimes so transpire. And

when the afflicted community asks what
it has done to deserve the calamity, this
is frequently the accurate answer. Why
the awful visitation of a civil war with
its loss of a million of lives and millions
of money; the infliction, too, upon the
North which enslaved no negroes? We
paid the penalty of fifty years of apathy
and the price of a sort of public conscience that mobbed Garrison and mur-
dered Lovejoy.

What have we, orderly, church-going,
industrious people, to answer for that
there are squalor and misery in the
hovels of Pennsylvania wage workers;
that hundreds of children recruit the
schools of vice in the streets of large
cities; that drunkenness goes on in-
creasing with the population; that dens
and dives fester in our great cities; that
disreputable elements come to the front
in our ward politics? We have no hand
in the bringing about of these matters;
the contrary, if anything.

Our responsibility is that we do not
fight and agitate and clamor against
the evil causes cropping out in such results. We cannot go off apart from our
brethren and save our own souls. If we
want to divest ourselves of responsi-

bility in and for those matters we must renounce the world. Living in it in any way, or co-mingling in its social or business activities in any degree, we are bound to recognize our partnership in the good and evil all about us, and do our duty in the premises.

**Theological Insularity.** THE English writer of verse, Coventry Patmore, is credited with the following utterance: "The world has always been the dunghill it is now, and it only exists to nourish, here and there, the roots of some rare, unknown and immortal flower of individual humanity. The holier and purer the small aristocracy of the true church becomes, the more profane and impure will become the mass of mankind." In other words:

"God bless me and my wife,
My son John and his wife,
Us four and no more."

Patmore, of course, counts himself, his wife, and his son John, among the small aristocracy of the true church.

This species of theological insularity is not new. The "chosen people" had it bad. The Moslems displayed it in their conquests. The "believer" was "God's son" — the Christian was a "dog." The Puritans resolved that they were the saints and the rest of the world was their's to plunder.

We see this spirit applied on the missionary side of the church. Christ told His apostles to go forth and preach the gospel to the whole world. Christianity was to be no monopoly. No "corner" was to be made on Salvation. The apostles had the spirit of the Messiah. When it came to a question of legislating a Jewish regulation into the discipline of the church they reasoned against it; no needless restrictions or burdens, repressive to the growth of Christianity, were to be created. So Christianity spread over the world under the preaching of apostles and saints, a study of whose lives discovers their singular breadth of view and tact of tolerance.

But a narrower kind of Christianity has always existed. We have had in all ages good men, apparently fearful that heaven would be uncomfortably overcrowded for them if Christianity were too widespread. They wish the society of Paradise to be quite select. Having a good thing in the gospel, they argue, we should keep it to ourselves. By hunting out heretics, engineering schisms and formulating new restrictions and regulations we can gradually freeze out hundreds of thousands of our fellow Christians. Then there will be more room for us lucky chosen people in heaven, and more of our, not as fortunate neighbors, will have to go to hell. Hallelujah! And it's a material fire down there, too!

**Ideas in the Pulpit.** ONCE upon a time a whole school of able preachers came to the Catholic Church as a result of a movement in Oxford University. The accession of Newman and his disciples "dealt a blow to the established church under which she still reels," said Disraeli; and the impetus in every line of thought and effort to the Catholic Church, from this accession, was correspondingly great.

Newman himself was not a preacher in the ordinary sense; he usually read his sermons in an even tone of voice and without gesture; but the preacher in the modern sense may be a writer of pamphlets: in fact, the German bishop, Von Ketteler, once said that if St. Paul came among us to-day to fulfill his mission he would be a journalist.

The Oxford movement, as a preaching force, gave strength to the Catholic Church in this: that it was an organized school of ideas, backed by earnestness and learning. If we are to have a renaissance of the preacher—as distinguished from the ecclesiastical manager (and both are useful)—we must look for it in something of the conditions which generated the Oxford movement: a strong seminary or university of learning, officered by a learned faculty, among whom are two or three men of the stamp of great teachers like Arnold or Newman, or of the apostolic mould like Manning.

Contact with such men, in the acquisitive stage of mental development, is not only education, but inspiration. It is as important to get the spirit of a university into the soul as its learning into the brain. The presence and influence of a master mind—giving new forms to old truths and fresh adaptations to the wisdom of the books, putting the life of to-day into the learning of yesterday, engendering the enthusiasm which glows from ideas which crave for action—this is the prime condition. And it is not the elocutionist nor the phrase-monger that is needed, nor whose lack has left the pulpit where it is; the rattling of dry bones in theatrical tones or the utterance of polished common-places with unctious gusto will not meet the requirement.

St. Paul, homely and under-sized, with a harsh voice, and Peter the Hermit, gaunt and ungainly, were the preachers of their days, because they had a message to announce, and they knew it, and would tell what they had to tell, even if they ran up against death and destruction in the task. And the people listened, as they will listen "to any Sermon or Sermo when it is a Spoken Word meaning a Thing and not a Babblement meaning Nothing."

**Repairs on the Church.** OUR church architecture is mediæval. It is a thing of time—not of eternity. We call it Gothic. All other relics of the Goths have gone, save a fragment of their literature. But the world has continued to copy their architecture. Not through any reverence, however. Simply for its grandeur—its spiritual effect, its great associations.

In the things of time there must be reason and utility as well as beauty. The life we lead will not in all things submit to be ruled by the tomb, nor by ideas that came from brains, now dust. The strong, virile society that *is,* demands that the world about it shall conform to its tastes and its needs. Those manifold agencies that minister to the moral and material wants of the people must evince a power of adaptability, or go down forever. Truth is unchangeable, but the language in which it is uttered changes and grows. Truth is unchangeable, but its clothes follow the fashion, or Truth is false to its own value in being indifferent to the duty of self-propagation.

Now, those great buildings that man has entitled by a more ambitious name than any palace or tower of his craft—"houses of God"—are not too sacred to get beyond the law of adaptation. The external church may well typify by its architecture the unchanging nature of the Gospel and the great lineage of years that (of all existing things) belongs to the Christian religion. The first Christian church was the Stable of Bethlehem, and if fidelity to the past were the true purpose, we should never get beyond that. It is not the external that we must look to, nor the symbolic. Utility is the thing. If beauty and symbolism and grandeur can be added, it is well; if not, we must sacrifice them.

Moderns have sometimes spoiled the chaste loneliness of the Gothic church by placing a school house adjoining; or even by filling its basement with the desecration of blackboard and spelling book. We may go further and add to the church other accessories demanded by the time that is—though unheard of in the time that was. We may not put our school into the church. We may keep the building dedicated to worship separate and alone. But we may put other institutions which elevate the social life of the people side by side with the church and school as influences that go with the work of the modern church. In so doing we may mean no disrespect to the Goths or the Vandals. Our meaning is solely that the concern of the living Church is with living men, and not with dead barbarians. We suffer no loss of fine feeling when we put heirlooms on the shelf; and hasten to take up present and pressing duties.

# THE GOSPEL FOR THE POOR.

Moral
Sanitation. In an old novel called "The Anti-
quarian," a fishwife, named Maggie, re-
plies to Mr. Oldbuck's criticism of
dram-drinking:

"Ay, ay—it's easy for your honor,
and the like o' you gentle folks to say
sae, that hae stouth and routh, and fire
and fending, and meat and claith, and
sit dry and canny by the fireside—but
an ye wanted fire, and meat, and dry
claise, and were deeing o' cauld, and
had a sair heart, whilt is warst ava, wi'
just tippence in your pouch, wadna ye
be glad to buy a dram wi't, to be eild-
ing and claise and a supper and heart's-
ease into the bargain, till the morn's
morning?"

What reply is there to this which will
convince the proponent? Drink is the
cause of misery and misery is the cause
of drink. We cannot expect the poor
to furnish all the examples of moral
heroism and self-restraint. Their condition is a state of temptation. On
every side temptation appeals to them

in the words of Romeo to the poor
apothecary:

"The world is not thy friend nor the world's law,
The world affords no law to make thee rich,
Then be not poor, but break it and take this."

When there was a famine in Ireland,
one section of the British people raised
a fund to buy Bibles. And they offered
the starving people books instead of
bread. There are ways in which this
mistake is repeated in a milder manner. When, for instance, we depend
altogether upon Faith and preaching
for the poor; and do not care how they
live so that they furnish examples of
"edifying deathbeds."

The aim of practical and religious
well-doing should be to remove temptation.

Whatever will improve the worldly
condition of the poor will improve their
spiritual condition. Better houses, better sanitation, better wages, steadier
work, savings banks, and those legisla-
tive measures which may be termed
"Christian socialism" are all praise-
worthy. We do not know but that this
is the way it was designed to have the
gospel preached to the poor.

MANY pious people who eat good dinners and sit by warm firesides have the phrase, "the poór are always with us," in their mouths for a totally different purpose than the Divine Teacher intended.

It does not mean that poverty is a sanctified state. Nor does it mean that misery and distress are insurmountable.

We find rich bad people and poor good people; but the general law connects poverty with sin, and comfort with virtue. There would be little avarice without want, little injustice without greed, and little intemperance without improvidence.

The influence that improves a people's worldly condition is almost certain to improve their spiritual condition. The reign of religion among hovels and tenements exists, in spite of the surroundings, in protest against them and in opposition to them. The reign of religion among peaceful hamlets and prosperous farms exists in harmony with the salubrious environment, and assisted by its healthful atmosphere.

To build solid piles of masonry dedicated to Christian worship and to pay through years of appeal and effort a universal indebtedness thereon, is one line of church work rendered imperative by the conditions of a new country and immigrant congregations. To institute great devotions, grand revival of religious fastings and public prayer, may be a most salutary and wise direction to lead the thoughts of the pious and faithful members of the congregation.

These directions of church effort, however, are only a few of the many functions which the Church discharges. The former is merely a preparation for work; the latter is a species of work which reaches only a limited number, and assists those who are already safely entrenched in the spirit and knowledge of their religion.

Lessons of frugality, sobriety and intelligence are a part of the Church's function. Throughout the middle ages the Church was a civilizing agency, leading in all reforms. The civilizing influence of the Church ought to continue in the nineteenth century. Civilization should not and can not properly lead the Church, but Christianity ought to lead civilization. What the masses in our average congregations most need is the right kind of civilization. They need it badly—the young people quite as much as the old. The Church is the center of true civilization, and, as a positive influence in advocating temporal comfort, decency and social elevation, is merely doing a duty that it began to take up in the days of the Cæsars.

A Civilization of Water. IN the early ages of the Christian Era the missionaries began, and accompanied their work of conversion by a work of civilizing. They cured the people of their ferocity, discouraged carousals and beastly diversions, and imparted a knowledge of the arts.

The barbarian was convinced of the virtue of frequent ablutions. Cleanliness prepared the soil for the reception of truth. The nomadic habits of the Pagan were gotten rid of it. He became an agriculturalist and a man of peace.

The early missionaries succeeded well. The civilization they spread was only an introduction to the Gospel.

Wherever a like policy has been pursued it has also succeeded. The Jesuits made millions of Christians in China, largely because they could teach the Celestials the geography of the heavens as well as the heavenly faith.

The modern missionary has a stratum of barbarism to penetrate in every city of Europe and America. There is a multitude of the great un-washed—savages nesting in the bosom of civilization. Moral influences, only, can reach or regenerate them. The modern missionary must civilize them as a prerequisite to Christianizing them. They must be cleansed exte-riorly and interiorly. Water is the means of attaining both kinds of clean-liness, and water is the civilization that must be preached. The public bath and the undiluted beverage are lines of missionary effort which go before much permanent Christianity. To neglect them is like expecting that a savage nation can be a Christian nation.

**After Dinner Charity.** WHO doubts that the recurrence of Thanksgiving Day does the nation good? We are advised, while we feed liberally to feel generously. The good nature of the gourmet, however, has little merit. It is merely an aid to

digestion. The finest words of charity
have been blocked out by grinding,
grasping rhetoricians, whose record of
giving is the only thing about them
that might blush—if seen. It is a
species of unthinking charity that re-
gards the poor one or two days of the
year, and forgets them the rest of the
time. Our after dinner, fashionable
charity is very much akin to the infan-
tile thoughtlessness of the little
princess, who, hearing it said that "the
people starve for want of bread," asked
"why don't they eat cake, then?"
Christmas and Thanksgiving are "the
cake days" of the year. We send turkey
to the poor and virtually absolve ourselves from any further solution of the
problem. It is a matter that well-fed
people prefer not to contemplate, except
as an addendum to fashion or as an aid
to digestion. The novelist of New
York society, Edgar Fawcett, says in
a magazine article: "It seems to me
that we touch the very horrible center
of this unassuaged social sore when we
state that most of our well-placed
women, who could aid their kind, will
not really aid them, and that they are
bored unspeakably by even the small,

dainty profferings of time and pin money which the modish churches they attend demand that they shall exploit."

Charity has been considered too much as an accomplishment and too little as a duty. A thing of generous impulse, it has, less than any other of the great functions of social life, come under the control of a scientific development. Its constitution and by-laws, its philosophy, its evolution, have not even been begun. It is a thing of fits and starts, full of clap-trap in its manifestations, liable to uncharity and injustice in its operations, vulgar in its methods of money getting and perpetually prostituted as a panderer to selfish and hypocritical natures.

Mediæval Charity. IT may be questioned whether "charity" in the old sense has any place in the modern vocabulary. Yet the same kind feelings and merciful motives are present with the modern world. Progress has been accompanied by many mitigating influences; the penal codes, the penitentiaries, sanitary regulations, moral movements and a score of other facts attest this. At the same time there is not the spontaneous, free giving that characterized other ages.

The modern world dislikes the beggar. It abominates poverty. It would rather blame the mendicant than relieve him. It withholds bread until it satisfies itself as to the worthiness of the petitioner.

This disposition may not be as charming as the free and lavish charity of other days, but it is really preferable in the end.

One source of poverty and beggary and misery has been the ease with which improvidence and intemperance could shift their burdens on the prudent, sober and industrious portion of the community. Doubtless there exist, to-day, organizations and establishments which assist improvidence by doing the begging in its stead. We refer to charity, organized on the mediæval, as opposed to the modern idea. The gist of criminality in many things which are *mala prohibita* lies in the evil they do to society. In this sense improvidence and intemperance are criminal facts, and it is but just that they experience their natural penalties. Indiscriminate charity does not recognize this, and the result is that the improvident class may go on with their excesses, thoroughly assured that their orphaned children will in the end be better fed and sheltered than the children of the thrifty workingman in the tenement quarters.

Charity, in its broadest sense, is the sum of all the virtues, and it can exist in its plentitude where there is no poverty and no necessity of giving. If men were just to their brother men—alms-giving would be unnecessary all around.

**Education in Giving.** SYMPATHETIC charity shelters the orphan and nurses the sick and wounded in great hospitals. Intelligent charity builds schools and lecture rooms and institutes for young men in the cities, and creates influences that conflict with the bad habits of society.

Sympathetic charity is mediæval. Intelligent charity is modern. The modern world has improved mediæval methods, as it should do. And it is no reflection upon the great good in mediævalism to say that as the world has grown older it has learned something. It has put more science and less impulse into its charity. Though intelligent charity may not be as beautiful as sympathetic charity, it is many times more useful.

Sympathetic charity is pathological —it waits for the ills and treats the disease. It picks up the waifs and wrecks of society; its hospitals and reformatories and asylums have no connection with the healthy current of the community's being.

Intelligent charity is hygienic. Its ounce of prevention is always worth a pound of cure. But just as the doctor, whose timely advice saves us from grievous disease, has less glory than the physician who brings us safely through a dangerous illness, so intelligent charity has less of the glamor of benevolence, but more of the substance, than sympathetic charity. It is in direct communication with the wholesome currents of life in the community's being, and exercises a strongly formative influence. Its schools teach creeds; its lecture rooms breed opinions; its institutes for young men give it the control of the future.

The state ought to take care of the functions usually discharged by sympathetic charity, and voluntary charity should direct itself to the hygienic works of benevolence. Our education in giving is largely neglected, and we are too much controlled by societies having their origin in non-modern conditions and which impose their choice of beneficiaries upon us. We wait to be asked; we do not choose before giving.

In a special locality, which element has the better hold on the future—that which builds a non-sectarian hospital or that which builds a Young Men's Christian Association hall? — that which spends its energies on building an asylum that competes with the State asylum or that which builds lecture rooms and lyceums? The one element concerns itself with the dead or decaying membranes of the body politic;—the other infuses itself into the healthy life blood of the living community.

**Brains and Heart.** "MALICE, prepense and aforethought" deepen and blacken the crime that follows. The deed is more cruel, more malignant and more diabolical.

It is a finished piece of villainy. It

corrodes and festers.  It spreads itself like an epidemic of hell.  Felony done upon the impulse may end with the act. There are no consequences.  The crime is blotted out in its own horror.  But the effects of premeditated evil remain.

The law of good and evil is the same in this respect.

Calculated well-doing is ten times as beneficial as impulsive well-doing. Impulsive generosity is a fine trait but calculated benevolence is much finer. Charity and alms-giving are good; but, with greater intelligence, comes a demand for a higher sort of charity. The creation of systems and forces which are charitable in their effects is the best phase of modern charity.

That kind of well-doing which unites brain and heart, which joins intelligence with goodness, is the desideratum.

# AMERICANISM.

**What Is Americanism?** WITH respect to the five foreign-born millions, settled in the United States, and their ten million children, the phrase "Americanism" has several special meanings — some of them wrong, most of them right and commendable.

There is intolerant and irreverent Americanism. It must be remembered that the German, the Frenchman and the Italian are not barbarians; they have been accustomed to a civilization of their own. Americanism cannot impose itself upon them. They came here to enjoy liberty; and they have ballots to cast and some choice to exercise. Blatant Americanism is vulgar, and when it becomes hysterical over its own unaccepted blandishments it is ridiculous as well. All organizations of the Know-Nothing kind, flying a flag of proscriptive Americanism, have found a truer Americanism up in arms against them.

In the following respects the phrase "Americanism" has a special and commendable meaning for foreign elements here settled:

1. Fealty to the democratic form of government.

2. An appreciation of the necessity of educating the people; and a thorough reliance upon the eventual wisdom of an intelligent democracy.

3. Opposition to all tendencies represented by such expressions as "the higher class," "the ruling element," "the American aristocracy," "the plutocracy."

4. Belief in the right of every man to make the most of his opportunities, to pitch his ambitions as high as possible, to better his condition, to rise above his station, to question and rebel against all conventional opinions which hold him down.

5. A conception of good citizenship as something based on Christian morality. Hence, an insistance on character and integrity in public officials and a desire for purity and honesty in politics. Necessarily this position must tend to a dislike for such influences as saloonism and semi-political corporations.

6.  A natural result of the feeling of fraternity, which grows out of the equality of every democratic community, is a desire for common standards, common customs and mutual confidence among neighbors.

For this reason Americanism is prone to be anti-masonic.  It dislikes political vereins and clans organized upon the basis of nativity; it is offended with customs of a foreign aspect which crop out too loudly upon the quiet of the American Sunday.  That some of the ministerial brethren have spoken hysterically on this subject, does not deprive it of its essential merits; a brass band, escorting a Turn-Verein past a Methodist church on Sunday morning, is certainly an invasion of the fitness of things.

The feeling of fraternity may at times menace individual liberty, with its plans for a common language, a common method of bringing up children and other common enterprises.  Nevertheless, the feeling itself, if it curbs its desire for over-legislation, is not reprehensible.

· The American of the future, whether his father came from Heidelberg with

Sigel, or from London with John Winthrop, has a right to whatever is best in the world's fair of ideas and customs. Tradition should not be a law against progress.

A Matter of Environment. HAVING higher ideals, American civilization rises superior in its realities to that of any other country. Even through the cobwebs of prejudice, one will have to acknowledge that a crowd of Americans selected at random are better gentlemen than a crowd of Europeans similarly selected. Their habits are cleaner; their morals, all things considered, are purer; and they are vastly more intelligent, more observant and more thoughtful.

We should neither exaggerate nor minimize the influence of breeding. The conditions which have surrounded the American community have been favorable. The man who went into the woods with his pioneer axe and there hewed his right to a home, was nature's nobleman. He could hardly help, considering his environment, to become a man of simple tastes, courageous methods, and with the American craving for schooling, a man of honest intelligence.

The conditions were different in the case of a peasantry constantly admonished to remain contented with their lot; disciplined to fill the ranks of standing armies like cattle driven to market; conscious that they were the lower order and social servants to a nobility. Or, if not in this category, a miserable, half-starved tenantry, dominated by a set of mean-spirited scoundrels, their landlords, and a prey, with very little moral or spiritual counter-effort, to habits of intemperance brought among them by their lords.

It is easy to perceive which environment favored the cultivation of higher ideals. While the greatest ambition of the plucked tenant or the subdued peasant was to keep the wolf from the door and maintain his station, the American woodsman or the young-man-come-West proceeded to grow with the growth of the country and to expand in desire and effort with the idea that his was an equal partnership in a great enterprise.

If there are impressionable elements of population in our midst, to which mass may they most advantageously be attached? Shall we send the currents of old world debility through them, or shall we tone them up with the electric vitality of youth, vigor, high hopes and advanced ideals? What do the doctors say? There are quacks who prefer the policy of segregation—shutting out the American sun as an irritant and the American atmosphere as a corruption. But the inevitable drift is the other way. The people naturally gravitate towards whatever is best in method and ideal. Not without quackery leaving its malign effects, for undoubtedly it has created great obstacles, caused much delay and occasioned considerable loss.

Beyond Their Station. THE "poor whites" are inhabitants of the middle southern tier of American states. A Scotch and Irish colonial ancestry is attributed to them, although it is probable that they draw quite as largely from the lower stratum of the English population. Often they are so devoid of energy and self-improvement that even the negro population fail to respect them. To the colored gentry they are "white trash."

Yet from this race came such men as Andrew Jackson and Abraham Lincoln, the greatest of the presidents since Washington and Jefferson. Obviously Lincoln reasoned in this way: "Because my parents and grandparents were born to this low social condition, it doesn't follow that I have to stay there. I see better things beyond me and higher things above me. Why should I not honorably go out of the house of Want and occupy the house of Have?"

The theory of certain sociologists is that Lincoln could not do this; his inferiority was bred in the bone; heredity was against him—the poor ambitions, nerveless purposes and wandering habits of his race created too overwhelming a balance of probabilities against his rise.

And the preachments of certain moralists bore in the same direction. Why should Lincoln want to rise? Why should he crave things above his station? Why should he not be content to stay down where his fathers and grandfathers were before him? Was he not flying in the face of Providence?

Lincoln does not appear to have real-

ized that Providence had any grudge
of this kind against him, and he certainly started out to disappoint the the-
ories of the sociologists. Studying law
by the light of a pine knot; passing
through the different phases of petti-
fogging in a country town; jostling
with all sorts of companionships, but
winning all by his homely wit, he rose
from one point to another, like a climb-
ing athlete, until he stood at the head
of the nation. Then it was said that
this "rail-splitting western poor white"
must be placed under the tutelage of
Seward and Chase, "men to the manor
born," or his administration would be
a failure; but in the way he had com-
pelled respect at the country bar, and in
the congress of the United States by
solid merit, by the great gift of unostentatious common sense, Lincoln was
more the chief of his cabinet by mental
superiority than any president since
Jefferson.

Now, there are other races concerning which sociologists are not so severe
as with the poor white; although narrow national prejudices exert a depre-
ciative influence. The Celt on the
banks of the Seine is the intellectual,

the political and social leader of civilized Europe; but the Celt on the Shannon has been a hewer of wood and a drawer of water from father to son—in some cases as long as grass grows and water runs.

Everybody understands that this result was not accomplished without the hydraulic pressure of compulsory ignorance, enforced poverty, legal robbery and martial rule exerted through centuries.

Cast upon the shores of the American states comes a poor emigrant—a wreck from a famine-stricken land in a fever-laden vessel—with his family. It is a passage from the struggle of the hovel to the hell of the tenement; of that emigrant family there survives but a boy of a dozen years. He drifts a waif into the interior of the states, doing the errands of theaters and the odd jobs of actors. But he does not appear content with his station. The right to rise above all adversity is inspired with the air he breathes. His advance is not rapid, but it is won step by step on the solid stairway of merit, until the elite of all the great cities crowd to hear him and pay tribute of applause to his dramatic power and finish; all America has known and honored Lawrence Barrett.

We are the architects of our own fortunes. Success is merely a question of how high we place our ideals and how earnestly we try to reach them. It is not in our stars, but in ourselves, if we are underlings.

Rise in the World. EVERY American is proud of the country's institutions; but the noblest and best of all our institutions, perhaps, is the hope which may be born in the breast of the bootblack or newsboy in the streets, that he may one day be president.

Class lines are forming here, it is true. And great fortunes and "first families" gangrene the democracy of fifty American cities, but the day is not yet past when even of the respected members of our United States senate an incident like the following may be told:

In 1882 a dinner party was given in New York city. Senator Davis, of West Virginia, sat at one end of the table, Senator Cameron, of Pennsylvania, sat at the other, and Gen. W. T.

Sherman at the head. The general began a reminiscence of his life by saying:

"When I was a lieutenant——"

"Come, now, Sherman," interrupted Mr. Davis, "were you ever a lieutenant?"

"Yes, Davis," he replied, "I was a lieutenant about the time you were a brakeman on a freight train."

"Well, boys," observed Cameron, "I don't suppose either of you ever cut cordwood for a living, as I did."

Now, when there is so much talk of improving the condition of the laboring population, it must not be overlooked that in case labor gets all it demands, the workingman will be a day laborer still.

A remedy to each individual man, better than eight hours or more pay, is to attempt to rise out of the ranks of labor altogether. Cease to be of that class if you can. You, thereby, better your condition and you leave a place vacant for the idle army of men who can't find work to do.

In this country no man is confined to "his station." Ambition is not a crime. It is the duty and the interest of every man to rise in the world; and rise he can if he enters upon the struggle with a will.

No station is too good for you. No station is beyond your strength or your capacity. Set no limits to your possibilities. Aim high, and when you have done your best be satisfied with the results.

This is the American style of settling the labor question: The laborer becomes a farmer, a storekeeper or an employer himself. Instead of casting his lot with Hungarian, Bohemian, Mecklenburg and Polish emigrants, who can't speak English and do not know the country, he takes advantage of his common school education and his English speech, and hires the Hungarians to work for him.

Of course, we must always have a laboring class, and it is the part of wisdom and benevolence to see that the cause of labor is promoted. It is at present, perhaps, the greatest duty we owe to society.

But no immutable law compels any man to remain a laborer forever. There must be rotation in the industrial world. If there is rotation, the yoke of labor will not be so burdensome as it might otherwise be. Under present hardships, there will be the hope of better times and more independent position. The workingman will not go to his daily toil as if he were

"At the mill with slaves,
Condemned to labor under Philistian yoke."

His existence will not be the drudgery of one who lives "from hand to mouth," but the energy of one who is making progress towards better things.

# THE PEOPLE KING.

Ordinary
People. WE are all educated. We vote. We
are sovereigns and peers. None of us
is so insignificant that he can be
trampled upon or pushed off the
common highway. Nevertheless what
ordinary, common place individuals
make up our vast centers of population.
What little originality of character!
what scarcity of true learning! what
lack of genuine nobility! what rarity
of real manhood, eighteen carats fine!

We have immense libraries stored
with tomes of weighty thought. But
the mob of readers devour the newspaper and the fiction. We have great
standing armies of teachers, but they
carry the mass of children no further
than their parents went. One generation halts where the other halted—at
the rule of three — at the half-way
house of common schooling.

In the brigades of wearied wage
workers, in the army of clerks leading
a hand-to-mouth existence, in the mob
of the grain pit, among the shysters and

quacks and semi-quacks of the professions, few rise above the ordinary role.

Mean and commonplace motives pre-
vail. Bread and butter is the absorb-
ing aim. Heads are turned by alder-
manic and mayoralty honors. Higher
laws or broader incentives are not
understood. They speak over the heads
of the populace, who talk in the style
and on the plane of philosophy.

"Fifty million of bores," thus has
Carlyle described this great people.
And Lowell finds us "the most com-
mon-schooled and the least cultured" of
races.

The inspired preacher has no chance
to be heard by our masses. The back-
woods revivalist, veneered or unve-
neered, catches the public ear most
quickly. Read the speeches that win
campaigns and tickle the sovereign
people. What sophistry, what dogmatism, what crude expression! We talk
of Shakespeare; by nine out of every
ten he is never read; by ninety-nine out
of every hundred he is never admired or
understood. We assume to arrive at
religious opinions; but with what
absence of research; with what lack of

close, earnest, thorough going contemplation and reasoning!

Taking people as they are, we must lay hold of the commonplace, in words and methods, to move their minds and influence their actions. They are not without their saving virtues. Whatever is plain, direct and honest, they like. The force of justice is clear to them. They are not blind to forgiveness and mercy. Go-ahead-edness, courage, constancy and sincerity claim their respect and conciliate their favor. The scholar has often failed; the genius has not blossomed; the preacher has been a mere nonentity and the philosopher a do-nothing, simply because each and all have not felt or known that the world is full of ordinary people.

A Lesson in Ethics. "WHAT is democracy striving for? What is the franchise worth to the masses if they sell their votes for beer? What is the self-government of cities worth if its features are municipal extravagance, willful waste in administration and bossism in political machinery?"

"Give us the net results to good gov-

149

ernment, to popular virtue and intelligence, to progress and civilization!"

We have to admit that frequently democracy gives us bad city administrations, and that if the test of the best government were that which is best administered, aristocracy and monarchy could often show better results. In the pandemonium of a caucus, and in the bribery and debauchery of a political canvass, it sometimes seems as if the people were getting very little good of it all; that it were better for them if they had no votes to be bought or beered for.

But there are other considerations. There is everywhere a large thinking and reading element who vote upon a careful judgment of the issues involved. The campaign does not succeed without the political speech—pitched, it is true, to a low grade of intelligence, but, nevertheless, an appeal to reason, and in that respect, an education. The ballot itself gives a sense of responsibility to the voter and makes him aware of his individual share in the commonwealth.

The mob may be loud and blatant, but it is not "dumb, driven cattle" at least. Out of it all comes much good. There are sentiments and convictions that at times sway the great democratic community in a way that seems to justify the stump-speaker's appeal to "this intelligent people." A wave of patriotism, a revulsion against political dishonesty, an uprising against monopoly, all speak well for the growing capacity of democracy. Blunder as it may, the People-King is the best ruler, for staying qualities, that society has yet found.

**Level Up.** WE wish to level up. If there is any levelling down to be done, it should transpire with the ulterior end of levelling up. To crush aristocracies is levelling down, but the ulterior purpose is raise the democracy. Consequently, the "levelling down process," so often complained of in democratic movements, is really part of a beneficent plan. Good men have held the theory that aristocracies are both desirable and inevitable. They have argued that social, educational and political institutions should be shaped accordingly. Here is their programme:

151

" To do away with social unrest and discontent, let the lower classes be taught that it is divinely ordered they should occupy their station; to aspire beyond the social rank of their parents is sinful. The professions are for the children of the middle class. Higher education should not be open to the poor. Too much education is not desirable for the masses. The civil service of the state should be recruited as largely as possible from the better class. Trade unions are pestiferous. Those who prate about social equality are demagogues. All efforts to improve the condition of the lower classes are futile. 'The poor we will always have with us.' It is fore-ordained that the good things of earth are for the few, and that toil and tribulation are for the many. Otherwise this world were not a place of probation. It is but natural for the wealthy to attempt making a Paradise out of earth; but for the many to seek to make this world pleasant is the manifestation of a dangerous kind of materialism."

Much of this programme needs but to be stated to be rejected. Its philosophy belongs to the sixteenth and seventeenth centuries, and the experience of the eighteenth and nineteenth centuries has exposed its fundamental fallacy. The American Republic is the most striking evidence in refutation. The leading purpose here is to advance in the mass and not in aristocratic castes. To this end there must be universal education. To this end, also, everything which will improve the tastes of the common people, everything that will shield them from brutalization or vulgarization, everything which will make their condition equal to the condition of the best class in Europe, is to be encouraged. Our solicitude is not for the future of the upper ten thousand. It concerns itself wholly with the welfare of the million who are not keeping pace. We may need popular reform and educational movements rather than higher institutions of learning. We need to provide for the mob rather than add to the comforts of prætorian guard.

And the lesson that is to be taught is the heritage, which every man has in the good things of the earth, if he but deserves them. Nothing is too good for the most ordinary creature. He has a right to hope for things that the Czar can not have. He has the right to feel himself of a company of citizen sovereigns, such as the Czar is hardly fitted to enter. No education is too high for the poor man's son. No career is too ambitious for him.

All of which sounds like spread-eagleism; but it is the simple truth of a happier epoch and a more Christian and brotherly theory of society. It is neither answered nor refuted by hitting it with an epithet.

# THE HARD FACTS.

A Balance
of Power.

UPON all great current questions with which public opinion is concerned there are weak men, assuming to lead, and proposing makeshifts. The labor problem demands attention, if it is to be touched at all, upon the basis which recognizes the mutual equality and independence of the laborer and the employer.

Weak men propose a makeshift which runs back to the middle ages for its idea: The employer shall be filled with a sense of his moral duty toward his workingmen. They, in their turn, shall respect the rights of his property. A very pretty program if it would work. It is the chivalric *noblesse oblige* regime brought down to solve the hard facts of the present problem, utterly ignoring the close competition which rules the industrial world of to-day and dictates the wages and treatment of workingmen; and utterly oblivious, too, of the unmitigated spirit of avarice which prescribes

"The plan
That he may get who has the power,
And he may keep who can."

The drastic solution of the labor problem demands frugality from the laborer and the stamping out by legislation of the chief influences which make him poor and keep him poor. Force is upon the side of the workingman, and in these days he is beginning to share also in the possession of Craft. Numbers, ballots, bullets and shrewdness will impel him to adopt effective measures. Legislation has its limitations, but its efficacy is hardly as narrow as doctrinaires and political economists have asserted. Legislation will not make a people virtuous, but it can stamp out primary schools of vice. It can not make the poor rich, but it can operate against the poor becoming poorer by operating against the rich becoming richer. It can check accumulation and promote distribution. It can regulate competition and promote co-operation. The presence of the railroad lobbyist and the monopoly agent in the halls of congress is a recognition by these practical money-making concerns that politics has a power over them which they will pay to escape. The capitalist may hold a whip over his workingmen in the vapory mine or in the crazy factory tower, but the enfranchised proletariat can rule capital with a rod of iron in the supremer factory of legislation. Whether it is policy for the employer to play tyrant in his shop, and whether it is policy for mere members to play despot in legislatures, is another thing. But if either holds off, its forbearance will be predicated on policy and self-restraint, not upon duty based on powerless moral sanctions. Capital will be disinclined to oppress labor only when it ascertains that, by combination and law-making, labor can retaliate; and labor will be disinclined to embarrass capital only when it recognizes that this will injure its own interests. Nothing is so promotive of peace as a balance of power; and is it toward something of this condition that the various events of the present labor movement are blindly and gradually, but, nevertheless, surely tending.

The Boycott Family. LABOR in its wrestle with capital frequently employed the " boycott," whereupon offended morality launched against this new word the artillery of its phrases: "un-Christian" and "un-American." It seems that the cold edge of much ethical teaching is reserved for poverty and the under-dog in the wrestle. The adage respecting the difficulty of rich men entering the kingdom of Heaven must have some reference to the exclusiveness with which the applied gospel is preached to the poor.

Now, here is an assemblage of godly rich men formed into a trust. It is not an In-God-We-Trust. Rather it is a devil's trust. It exists for the purpose of regulating the law of supply and demand. This is a euphonism for the mild purpose of getting more from the public for their productions than the undoctored market would yield them. Anon, a brother Christian, goes into the same business. He puts up his capital, and he is willing to put in his honest toil. He asks but a fair field and an even opportunity. This is promptly denied him. He is the chosen victim of a fiendish boycott. He experiences all the inexorable hatred of a malevolent clan. Even the poor privilege of a

place in the conspiracy to rob the public is denied him. This is but a single instance of the unconvicted, unanathematized boycott which moves in the best society and occupies a distinguished place in the synagogue.

How numerous the family of boycott are in the high places, moving under the name of Vanity, Exclusiveness, Upper Tendom, "the Four Hundred," with their purse proud manners and their unfeeling "cuts" for their social inferiors and poorer imitators; how the family crops out in politics under the name of Know-Nothingism or similar faction, or how it sets up in business as monopoly, credit and syndicate, the most casual observer must know. Yet all the raps are for that end of the family in blue jeans, carrying a tin pail or wielding a spade.

Cannot Use the Church. IT is not essential for the Church to be super-zealous in interposing in labor troubles, to instruct the workingmen that they have duties as well as rights, that contracts and property must be respected, and that there is a decalogue of "Thou shalt nots" which they must not transgress.

159

Bosses would like to have the Church do this whenever the industrial machinery gets out of order—disordered partly through the greed of the bosses themselves. They would like to have the Church do police duty for them and preach to their pecuniary profit.

The Church has lectured the workingman very frequently. But the Church must be impartial. The capitalists and bosses stand in need of lecturing, too. Their avarice, their stock watering, their tariff jobbery, their wage cutting, their trusts, their arbitrary shutting down of factories, and their dozen other capital sins, need to be fitly rebuked.

And one way, and a most efficient way, of rebuking them is to let them take the consequences of their own avarice, unwisdom and injustice. If they sow the wind we do not see why the whirlwind should be anathematized for them. Experience is the best teacher for rich fools as well as for poor fools. If men pushed to the verge of starvation rebel, there is no reason why the Church should be brought in between them and the oppressors as a sort of buffer. Let the wealthy man's

church tell him his duties as well as his rights. The poor man's church is continually doing that for the working-man.

> "Man's inhumanity to man
> Makes countless numbers mourn."

It is not the masses, but the classes, who are inflicting most of the wrong. True, the masses need instruction so that they may be kept in order, but much more frequently the classes need instruction, and much less frequently they get it. The French peasantry were told to be submissive to their superiors and contented with their station, but the nobility brought out their pretty maxim, *noblesse oblige,* only for ornamental occasions. When the delayed tempest came the Church could not allay it—the altar came down with the throne in the social crash that ensued.

The Church is not of, nor for, the things of this world. If the experience of history, if the common sense of society, if the courts, if the trade unions, if the interests of commerce itself, if the police can not keep the peace, then it is not the Church's

funeral. Society may go under, but the Church will stay. The sooner this is appreciated the better for all parties. The Church is not here to play policeman for either kings or labor lords.